STINGING SILENCE
BY
E.A. DARL

Cover Design by Greg Simanson

Edited by Judith Docken

EPUB ISBN 978-1-989022-06-1

EPUB ISBN 978-1-989022-06-1 (AS PART OF THE SILENT LANDS CHRONICLES BOXSET #1-4

PAPERBACK ISBN 978-1-989022-14-6

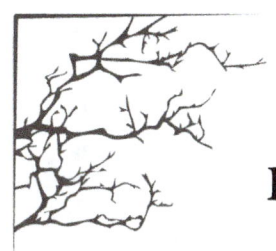

DEDICATION

We dedicate this book to all of our earlier adaptors, who have dived into the series with excitement and fervour.

We hope our words inspire you to think about the world around us. Humanity and nature walk this planet side by side, and neither can exist without the other.

Well, maybe nature can. It is humanity that is running amok, out of pace with the reality of life.

There is room for us all to co-exist. But if one or the other is to fail, it may just be humanity that goes extinct for being too blind to see and too stupid to care.

Time will tell for all.

-The lovely ladies of E. A. Darl

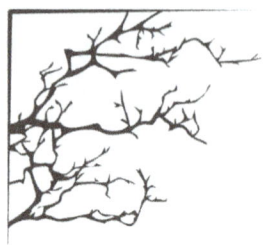

Chapter 1
Kidnapped

THE DRONE OF THE CESSNA'S single engine vibrated the cushion, shaking Mitch awake with a groan of pain. He moaned at the sharp stabbing sensation that throbbed at the back of his head. He reached back with his right hand to examine the lump he was sure stuck out of his hair but could not as his hands were bound in front of him. His eyes opened to a blue leather pilot's chair, separated from him by a glass partition. The grey head of the pilot swiveled to the side, glancing into the back seat. Mitch caught sight of a curling grey mustache adorning his upper lip. The co-pilot's chair was empty.

"Relax, Mitch. There is no place to go, and any attempt to attack me will result in both of us dead. Enjoy the flight. We will be landing in about ten minutes."

"Where are you taking me? What is the meaning of this?" Mitch rolled onto his back and held his bound hands up in front of his face. The tie had cut deep into his left wrist, and a trail of smeared dried blood ran down his arm. An inaudible growl caught in his throat.

"You have been dabbling in things you shouldn't have. We have some questions for you. That is all. I can feel it when you roll on that seat. Now lay still unless you want to unbalance this plane."

Mitch ignored the advice, glaring at his captor. "Who are we? Who are you?"

"All will become clear when we land." The pilot turned back to face the windscreen and ignored Mitch. It was a clear dismissal. He had no intention of passing on further information. To prove the point, he switched on his console, and suddenly the plane was filled with the sound of an old rock song. The ADF receiver had zeroed in on the unmanned radio station signal that played continuously from the station located in Melona. Mitch knew it was the case because he had listened to it for years. The song always skipped at a particular interval, and, sure enough, as soon as it reached that spot, it passed over an entire verse of the song. He smiled, know knowing his approximate location. He craned his neck to confirm the location of the sun in the sky.

We are flying northwest over Melona. If we do not lose the signal, then I know we are within a hundred-mile radius of the town, and in that direction lies...the government warehouses. A frisson of alarm skittered down his back. *Damn! /have they found me out?*

The plane droned on, flying into the darkening sky as the sun coursed through its daily track. The music faded away, and Mitch's heart sank. They were going further than he thought. Perhaps it was the government, but his first guess proved wrong. Mitch shifted onto his side and his eyes closed, lulled by the hum of engine and the need to escape from his splitting headache.

He awoke to the sensation of the burlap sack being pulled down over his head once again. He was hauled up off the seat and out of the plane, stumbling for a second as he gained his balance. Hands grabbed either arm and led him away. Through the bottom of the sack, he could see the runway was grass, not pavement. A rural landing strip, he guessed. He did not resist his silent escort. When he heard a car door open, he paused. A hand on the back of his neck forced him to duck inside the open doorway, and he settled onto the back seat of a car. The door slammed, and the car engine purred to life and drove away. He tried to peer around under the sack, but suddenly it was pulled from his head. Seated beside him in the back of the Lincoln was the most beautiful woman he had ever seen. Regal, like a queen, she sat straight-backed, her nose wrinkling on her narrow, pale face.

It dawned on Mitch that he smelled like a bar fight without the booze, all sweat and blood and that undeniable stench of things gone sour. He also realized that he was parched, his throat drier than a spider's last meal.

"I apologize for my state of, uh, or lack of a recent shower. The express trip across the badlands had no rest stops," he croaked, leaning away from the woman.

She sniffed, tucking a stray strand of ebony hair ribboned with grey behind a delicate ear. She raised one brow and said, "Understandable. Give me your wrists."

Mitch held out his wrists. The woman pulled a knife from her pocket and sawed through the plastic strip. He winced at the pressure as she worked on the binding, which snapped, freeing his wrists. The relief mixed with fresh pain, and the cuts oozed. She dropped the restraints into a bag and handed him some baby wipes. Mitch washed his injured wrists, depositing the soiled sheets in the bag.

"Hold out your hands again." He did as commanded.

"Who are you?" asked Mitch. As his voice croaked, her eyes met his. They were a vivid green. *I could drown in those eyes*, he thought, as she smoothed an antibiotic cream on the cuts and then wrapped a soft gauze around the wounds.

"I am Maria," she said simply. She taped the ends and then handed him a thermos of water.

Grateful for the cool liquid, he drank his fill before handing the mostly empty thermos back to her.

"Keep it," she said, ignoring his attempt. She settled back in her seat, gazing out the window. "I apologize for the rough treatment, Mitch. We did not intend to hurt you. Only secure your cooperation. They," she waved a manicured hand at the out-of-sight plane, "were meant to bring you, regardless of your wishes, but they were a little too enthusiastic in their instructions."

"You still know more about me than I do you. Are you government?" At the negative shake of her lovely head, he said, "A spy for a faction? The leader of a faction?"

She hesitated at his words. He could see that she was struggling with what to say. "Not in the way you think." She watched the passing scenery out the window for a moment then turned back to Mitch with a sigh. "A long time ago, my identity was changed to protect all involved," she said in a quiet voice. "I go by Maria Mainz now, but I was born Ellen Maria Gainsborough. I believe you have been looking for me."

Mitch stared at her in complete shock. *Avalon and Alexa's mother?*

Her eyes flicked over to him, gauging his reaction, and then she looked away, embarrassed.

"I don't know what to say. Believe me, this is a first. I searched for you for years! Every lead went cold. Every trail a dead end. I had the full might of the police department at my fingertips. We finally closed it down as an unsolved missing person's case." Mitch shook his head. "Was this all staged? Was the kidnapping fake? Was your disappearance a fraud? *You left your children behind to starve!*" Mitch's voice rose in anger. *"Avalon, Alexa. How could you abandon them like that?"* The last words came out in an angry shout, and Mitch heard the click of hammer on a gun being cocked, ready to fire. He made himself relax, pushing himself back into the seat, but still his fists clenched with anger.

Ellen had tensed at his tirade, but she hadn't turned around. At the click of the hammer however, she leaned forward and put a hand on the shoulder of the man in the driver's seat.

"Don't, Albert. He has the right to be angry. He does not mean to harm us." She squeezed his shoulder.

He tensed under her touch then took his right hand off the gun and placed it back on the wheel. He did not relax his guard. Angry black eyes stared at Mitch from under heavy dark brows, reflected in the rear-view mirror.

Mitch's narrowed eyes moved between the pair. "You have a lot of explaining to do, both of you. Is this why you have gone to such lengths to get me here? So you could talk to me in secret away from prying eyes?"

Albert answered his question. "Yes. You are being brought to our hideout. It also doubles as the headquarters of the SOS. We have questions to ask you, but we couldn't risk being seen in the open, not for you, not for the kids. The world must believe we are dead."

He spun the wheel, taking a rutted lane off the quiet road and meandering back through the underbrush to the base of a railroad trestle. Mitch's eyes wandered the scene, trying to figure out where they were headed. It looked more like a good place for an execution than a hideaway. His gaze settled on Ellen's rigid profile. She was the very likeness of Avalon, a child she had not seen in five years.

"You look just like Avalon," he said. "She is a miniature you."

Ellen's face turned toward him. Unshed tears, held firmly in check, sparkled in her eyes. "Thank you. I am sure she is very beautiful." She turned away again to stare out the window as her husband steered the car underneath the trestle and straight toward a wall of stone. "How are they?"

Alarmed, Mitch did not hear her reply. Instead, he cried out as he ducked behind the front seat, but the anticipated impact did not occur. The car shot right through the wall. Heart beating very fast, his rationale caught up to his instincts and he sat up.

"What the hell was that?" he gasped. They were inside a cave hollowed out of the hillside. The large metal structure could have housed the plane they had flown him in, not unlike the silo facility he had just left. People in farming gear and lab coats moved to and fro, pushing carts loaded with burlap sacks or driving tractors hauling plows or seeders. No one paid them any heed. They went about their duties unconcerned about the stranger in their midst.

"A hologram. It is a very expensive piece of deception. We stole it from the government," said Albert.

The car eased to a stop by a door. Albert put it into park and then turned around to look him full in the face for the first time. Lines of worry had dug deep furrows into the once youthful face and his hair was liberally sprinkled with grey.

"Welcome to the secret facilities of the SOS, the 'Seeds of Survival' initiative. It is our most important facility." Mitch took a deep breath to slow his racing heart then nodded acceptance of the welcome. He had found them, or rather they had found him. Avalon and Alexa would be so happy. *Their parents were alive!*

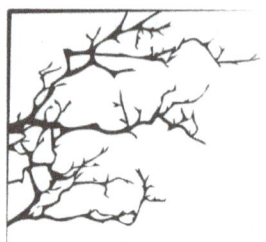

Chapter 2
The Initiate

AVALON LAUNCHED ALL one hundred twenty pounds of enraged female from the couch like a rocket, lunging with outstretched hands to grab Magnum's throat. All Avalon wanted was to choke the girl where she stood. She was tired of being pushed, prodded, and goaded into reacting, yet here she was again, attacking the taunting teen.

Magnum laughed as Avalon bounced off the Plexiglass barrier and was tossed to the floor. She crossed her arms, her eyes glinting and lips twisted into a mocking smile. "She doesn't handle the drugs well, does she?"

Trench leaned up against the wall picking his nails clean with tip of his switchblade while watching Avalon rage. "You know, I wouldn't get on her bad side. That girl has some serious anger management issues. They might even be worse than yours."

Magnum stuck her tongue out at him and went back to smirking at the out of control Avalon through the safety of the Plexiglass. The room where they had secured Avalon was an old office space tucked off the back of the main kitchen. All furniture had been removed long ago, except for a rolling cot that they used as a place to crash and get some sleep. The window's blinds had been pulled up, giving a clear view out into the kitchen. They had moved the unconscious Avalon into the room and laid her on the cot after she had passed out from the branding. Trench had given her a shot of oxycodone to ease the raw pain of her burnt arm, and then they had wrapped the wound and left her to rest.

However, Avalon had awoken. Finding herself in the narrow cell-like room, she'd jumped to her feet and charged the window, screaming and raving about jail. She'd thrown herself over and over at the window, her face contorted with rage and a wild, insane light to her eyes.

"Uh-oh," Magnum had said and then wedged a chair under the doorknob, effectively locking Avalon inside. "Trench, we have a problem!" she had yelled over her shoulder, bringing him back to her side.

Again and again, Avalon hurled herself at the window. Magnum watched the small girl, fascinated by the desperation underlying her aggression. The attacks had a feral quality about them. The girl was acting like a caged bear she had seen once at a zoo. Feral and deranged at the same time. Avalon was extremely dangerous right now.

Most people who are hallucinating are dangerous purely by accident, as they do not sense pain. That is what the drug is for. To deaden pain. Who knew she'd have no ability to handle it, thought Magnum. *Weak.*

Avalon had given up on her direct attacks at the window and lay curled in a ball on the cot, cradling her sore arm. She had not moved for the last five minutes.

"Hey, Trench," Magnum called over her shoulder, "looks like she has fallen asleep again. What do you want to do now?"

Trench left off counting their food supplies and wandered back over to the window. "I will watch her. We are running low on just about everything. I need to you to do a foraging run. See if you can find another abandoned storage warehouse like you did last time."

"We got lucky, Trench. The warehouses are nearly always controlled by rival gangs. We'd have to fight our way in just to get a peek at what is inside of it. That last one was a fluke because it didn't look like a warehouse from the outside. I think it was a food bank or something originally. The outside was painted up like an auto body shop."

"Go back to that warehouse, and let's do a thorough sweep of it. Maybe there will be a clue to other food stashes across the city. We know they had more than one outlet. Take some help. And Magnum," he said as she stepped away from the window, "watch your back, OK?"

"Got it, boss!" She tossed him her usual smirk and left the kitchen.

Trench took the chair out from under the doorknob, opened the door, and carried it inside, setting it quietly on the floor beside Avalon. He sat down next to her and watched the slow rise and fall of her arm, cradled on top of her chest. She was indeed asleep. He hoped she was sleeping peacefully. His eyes traced the features of her face.

"You are a mystery, Avalon," he said softly to the sleeping girl. "Despite our talk of a little while ago, I sense you have more secrets than you shared. That's OK. I do, too. But you are one of us now. Be careful what you do. Do not force me to destroy you." He ran a hand over her hair then settled back in his chair by her bedside.

AVALON WAS HAVING THE strangest dreams. She was back in the jail in Melona, and then she wasn't. Mitch was there, and then it was a different man, the Firebrand gang boss. She had to get out, she couldn't stay, and both were holding her back. She moved her arm and cried out. It was on fire. They were burning her alive! She thrashed, and a hand grabbed her hand and soft words floated across her consciousness, soothing her frayed nerves and nerve endings. She drifted off once again.

This time, when she woke, she stared around at the puce-coloured walls with disgust. She'd hated this colour for as long as she could remember. Lighter rectangles spoke of pictures long gone. The ceiling was the same depressing pink as the walls. She turned her head, and she immediately cheered up. Trench sat in the chair beside her, his chin rest-ing on his chest, fast asleep. His arms were crossed. From Avalon's perspective, all she could see was his bulging bicep where it exited the short sleeve of his T-shirt. Avalon dragged her eyes away and sat up, coughing. The noise woke Trench, and he straightened, instantly awake. His eyes were wary.

"How do you feel?" he asked, dropping his arms to his knees. Dark crescents under his eyes hinted at his lack of sleep.

"Good. My arm is a little sore. Why?" She looked around the room. "Where are we?"

"This is an office space just off the main kitchen. We use it as a place to flop when we're tired. You have been here for a day."

Avalon frowned. "A day? Why would I need to be here for a day?"

"We gave you some medicine to help with the pain from the brand. You reacted badly. I have never seen such a reaction," said Trench.

Avalon scowled. "What did you give me?" she demanded. "I can't take most painkillers. I have bad reactions to them."

Trench laughed. "That is an understatement. You went berserk. Even Magnum was scared of you, although she'd never admit it."

The door opened. Cris stood in the entrance, her face thunderous. "I still vote for just putting her down. She is going to get us all killed with that temper. She," she pointed at Avalon, "is a liability to us all." Trench stood as Cris marched over and confronted him, nose to nose.

"Since you are so scared of Avalon, I am assigning you to her training. You will work alongside her and introduce her to our activities. If you get killed," he nodded toward Avalon, "I will know you were right." He put his finger under Cris's chin, raising her angry face to meet his. "But, I'd prefer if you both lived." He kissed her lightly on the lips and then left Avalon alone with Cris.

Cris turned triumphant eyes on Avalon. "Come on, you need a change of clothes before we hit the streets." Avalon got up and followed Cris out of the cubicle and through the back doors to a hallway, all the while wondering how she was going to stand being with this girl all day long. One or the other was sure to snap. One thing was clear, she had a dangerous rival in this girl, and it wasn't just over Trench's attention.

Not that I want Trench's attention, never that. Avalon squirmed internally. *I can lie to myself, but I always know it's a lie. Most inconvenient.*

Chapter 3
Comparing Notes

PEET PUSHED HIMSELF up off the couch, struggling to not move his leg any more than necessary, which of course was an abysmal failure. "Oww. Dammit. Ouch! Six teeth of a tooth fairy, that hurts!" he grumbled as he stumbled to Dr. Song's favourite chair.

Alexa laughed at his swear words, knowing he changed them for her. "Six teeth of a tooth fairy?" she giggled, grabbing a stool and dragging it over under his leg.

Peet scowled at the imp. "Do you really think they get all their teeth from youngsters like you? They steal them from adults too, you know. Although they hide it by posing as dentists. That is why you have to lie back in the chairs so far, so you can't see the bump of their wings under their lab coats."

Alexa howled with laughter. Peet hid his smile in his shoulder, unwilling to give up the game quite yet. He was glad to see her in good spirits after their flight from the government agents, getting shot by those selfsame agents, and then forcing her to drive his car. That either of them was alive was a miracle, and she deserved to laugh.

"That's not true, Peet! You are teasing me."

Peet replaced his smile with a wince and a groan, then mock glared at Alexa. "You think I am joking, do you? Why pull out teeth when they can make them? Answer me that one."

"They pull them out when you don't brush your teeth." Alexa grinned at him, assured in her knowledge of this matter. "Didn't you brush your teeth, Peet?"

"Of course, I did! Once every three months, as instructed by the tooth fairy, err, I mean dentist."

Alexa laughed. "No, no! You have to brush them every day! To keep the gremlins away." Alexa smirked, enjoying the childish game. Gremlins were much more fun than tooth fairies. She hadn't believed for a very long time, but it was fun to play along.

Peet ran his hand over his stubbly chin, frowning. "Gremlins, you say? Gremlins? Well, I suppose they could have been gremlins. They come in the middle of the night, right? Sometimes during the day too, if you are scared of dentists and have to sleep in the chair." He shifted slightly then said, "I will make you a deal. Next time you have a wiggly tooth, give it to me and I will stay awake to see who comes to get it. Deal?"

"Deal!" said Alexa, flashing her cheekiest grin around a mouth full of perfect teeth. "I am afraid you will lose this bet. I have all my adult teeth. I think you will end up losing some before I do." Peet grinned back, gap-toothed. Three teeth were missing in the front row. Alexa hugged him hard. "You are the funniest man I know! Even funnier than that cartoon duck. I can't remember his name, but we used to watch it on Saturday afternoons on TV when I was really little." Her smile faded as she remembered.

Seeing her mood changing, Peet said, "Well, are you going to get me a cup of tea? That is why you woke me up, wasn't it?" Her smile returned, and she scooted out of the room, calling for Dr. Song as she left.

Peet eased himself into a more comfortable position then picked up a magazine that sat on the side table. The title proclaimed it to be a science magazine, several years out of date. The cover featured a weathered old farmer, kneeling on one knee in a field and examining a withering plant. The soil beneath his boot was dry and cracked with huge furrows running in all directions. It had been many years since any farmer had attempted to plant crops under the naked sun. As the clouds had vanished and the drought deepened, farming had moved indoors to warehouses and ice rinks and sports facilities, any place where the environment could be controlled and moisture created artificially. Moisture collected from sweating pipes and air conditioning coils was meticulously collected, the water life-giving in a dying world. The headline on the cover proclaimed "Worst Drought in a Century Grips the Farming Heartland."

At that moment, Dr. Song shuffled into the room, carrying two cups of tea. Alexa walked carefully behind him carrying a plate of crackers. Seeing his patient sitting up, he smiled at Peet. "Well, it's about time you woke up. Your colour has returned. Good." He set the tea on the side table and took Peet's abandoned spot on the couch. "How do you feel?" Alexa placed the crackers beside the tea then skipped out of the room to return with a small jar of jam with a spoon stuck in it. She put it down beside the crackers then joined Dr. Song on the couch.

"As well as can be expected for recovering from a gunshot wound and no hospital nearby. I am grateful we are both alive. Alexa did a hell of a job getting me here." Alexa beamed at the praise.

"She is a smart girl. You must be very proud of her," said Dr. Song.

"She is not my daughter. She is the daughter," Peet hesitated slightly over the small lie, "of a friend." In actual fact, he had never met Alexa and Avalon's parents, as they had disappeared many years ago as a result of a government cover up and scandal that had resulted in the two girls being orphaned on their own farm and forced to live on the streets to survive. It was his personal belief that they were still alive and that their current host might be able to enlighten them to why the government abducted the two eminent scientists in the first place. "She is the daughter of Ellen and Albert Gainsborough," he said quietly.

Dr. Song's brows lifted in surprise, and then he glanced over at the child seated beside him. "You are quite the surprise, my dear." He focused back on Peet. "I do not believe that you were shot on purpose just to get access to me. I also do not believe in coincidences. I am thinking you were coming to see me anyways and just got shot along the way." At Peet's nod of affirmation, he grunted. "So then, tell me why you are here?"

"We found some information in the hospital records."

Dr. Song raised a white brow in question. "Found or stole?"

"How about we say acquired. You worked at the hospital for over thirty years. You know all the doctors who have been in and out of that facility. Yet there were two doctors on loan from the government about ten years ago who had no ID yet full access to all programs and services. They were studying some strange disease on a specialty basis, and the results were encrypted. The timing of this is suspicious in the extreme. It was only a short time later that the Gainsborough's went missing. I think you know what this is about, Dr. Song. I think it is why you chose to hide away from the world. I think you want everyone to forget you ever worked at the hospital."

Dr. Song stared at Peet. "I don't deny it. I wanted nothing to do with the hospital when I left. I retired and faded from view as quickly as I could. I live a peaceful, quiet retirement here. I prepared in advance for this time. I knew it was coming, you see. I knew the land was dying."

"How did you know? You are a medical doctor."

Dr. Song took a sip of his tea then stared at the swirl of leaves in the bottom of the cup, gathering his thoughts. "In the beginning, the signs were subtle. The doctors in the ER started dropping offhand comments about the poor diet of the patients coming through. Cases of scurvy and iron deficiencies were the early indicators that something catastrophic was occurring in the local food supply. The cases of severe nutritional deprivation and diseases related to these conditions, such as rickets and beriberi, multiplied until the trend was undeniable."

"What trend? What did you discover?" asked Peet.

The old doctor lifted his head. "Something was poisoning the food being handled and eaten by all of us. The food that was being grown was nutritionally deficient, and fewer people had access to healthy food. Something in the environment was affecting the food, but not just the nutritional value. The produce itself was coated in a toxin also, and those closest to the problem were the first to show signs of illness. The first cases came from the agricultural community, those doing the planting and cultivating and growing. Farm workers and farmers. Then we started seeing those who handled the produce becoming ill: grocery store employees and warehousers, truck drivers, cannery employees. The list goes on and on. Anyone who came in contact with the produce became ill. The plague acted like a virus, infecting all who came in contact with it, yet it was undetectable by the normal screening processes put in place by the Department of Agriculture's standardized testing."

"How do you know it is undetectable?"

"A government agricultural tester was one of the patients that came into the hospital in the second wave of illnesses that flooded into the hospital. He told me about a pandemic they were trying to contain but that was undetectable by their current methods. He had a bronchial infection that he thought he had acquired from working in one of the hot house greenhouses. This was back when they were still privatized operations. When I questioned him further about his exposure, he said he couldn't say anything more, that they were under orders to not talk about it to anyone on the outside. He had only come in because he couldn't breathe any longer. We did the usual work up on him and took X-rays of his lungs. He had tumors the size of my fist. He died within hours of arriving at the hospital. There was nothing we could do for him."

Alexa's sat with her mouth wide open as she listened to the adults talk.

Peet swore for real this time, forgetting she was there. He held out his arms. "Come here, Alexa." Alexa ran over to him, and he pulled her close to his side. "Don't you worry, you are safe. If you were infected, you would have died a long time ago. This is something that happened a long time ago, around the time your parents went missing. OK?" He gave her a little shake and smiled down at her. Her head bobbed acknowledgment. Over her head, he said, "Do the two unidentified research scientists have anything to do with the cases?"

"Yes. They were sent by the government to study the cases. They were not there to treat them, but more like scientists observing lab rats. They took most of the patients who showed symptoms away with them to be studied in a secure facility somewhere. We were happy to see them go, frankly. The last thing we needed was a hospital full of people who could not be treated. We did not question it overly much, believing at the time that the government had specialized help brought in just to handle the issue."

"The patients never returned though, did they? Are you aware of any who were cured?"

Dr. Song shook his head. "No. They all died in their care. We received copies of the death certificates so that we could close the hospital record, but that was it. We assumed the bodies were passed on to the next of kin."

"Did you ever figure out what was causing the disease? I mean, you must have had some thoughts around it. Was it something ingested? Airborne? Passed on by physical contact?"

Dr. Song shook his head. "No. The closest we came to a working theory centered on some pollen collected from the coveralls of the greenhouse worker. One of my colleagues put the pollen under a microscope as a joke, wondering if it was a hyper allergen. What he discovered was that the pollen was a thousand times sharper than regular glass shards. Every spike on the minuscule particle was a tumor waiting to happen."

"Did you report this?" said Peet, his voice sharp.

"To whom?" said Dr. Song, his voice equally as sharp. "*The government doctors?* They were the ones hiding the evidence! They took away every single person who presented themselves at Emergency, citing section this and section that. They were ready to shut down the entire hospital and turn patients away who were not part of this problem. They were willing to let people die in the ambulances lined up at the door! We had no choice." Silence filled the room. "But...it does not mean that we kept no records at all. We just didn't keep the type they can easily find."

Alexa piped up. "You wrote everything down. Computers are easy to copy."

Dr. Song winked at her. "That's right, Alexa. We made paper records and kept them in a very special place."

"Where?" she asked. Peet leaned forward to hear the answer better.

"Right here." Dr. Song got up and pushed the couch out from under the window. Lying flat on the floor underneath the sofa was a black leather hard-sided briefcase. He bent over and picked it up by its handle. "I assume this is what you were looking for, Peet?"

Peet nodded. "Thank God. Now we can get to work."

Chapter 4
Digging into the Truth

MITCH STRAIGHTENED, stretching his back to work out the tender kinks that were the result of his recent transportation experiences that had brought him to this spot. He followed the retreating backs of the Gainsborough's as they made their way deeper underground. After they passed the initial human traffic, the tunnel dove straight through the hill on which the south section of trestle rested and emptied out into a garbage heap. Mitch stopped dead in his tracks. The SOS was located in a dump? His nose wrinkled with the sulphuric smell of rotting vegetation and other odours that he struggled to place.

"Uh, why are you all parked on the edge of a garbage dump? This makes no sense."

Albert's faced creased into a thin smile. "It wasn't our choice, trust me. What you see is a garbage dump. What we see is evidence."

He led Mitch down between tall columns of wood laid on their sides like retaining walls. Garbage mounded up out of the top of the pile threatening to tumble down into the passage with a good gust of wind.

"I don't understand," said Mitch, frowning. "Care to elaborate?" He followed their silent forms, annoyed at the lack of communication. "You went to all the trouble to bring me out here to show me what?"

They took a right fork and then climbed a rough staircase made of leftover paint cans to the top of the pile. Mitch's head leveled then moved above the height of the garbage.

Lying in the midst of the pile of trash was a flattened section partitioned off by ropes. The area had been dissected into quadrants. Within each quadrant, masked and gloved people worked with brushes, tiny shovels, and water bottles to clear away the surface of the area.

"An archaeological dig? In a dump?" said Mitch in utter amazement. "You really believe you will find anything that old in here?" He gazed around at the trench they had just climbed out of, and then it dawned on him how much work they had already completed. As he gazed out over the dump, over the acres of garbage, he realized the retaining walls were sites already dug to bedrock. This excavation had been going on for years.

"Twenty years to be exact," said Ellen. Mitch turned towards Ellen at the sound of her voice. He hadn't realized he'd spoken the words out loud. "We first heard of the deposits back in our college days. The hills around Melona show evidence of an ancient marsh that was pushed upward by seismic activity, and the remains of dinosaurs had been found, on and off, for centuries. We used to volunteer for those outings, to go scavenging for fossils containing dinosaur bones. Those were fun days. Then the government stepped in and stopped it."

Albert leaned against the temporary fencing, studying the scene. "It was under the guise of protecting our national heritage, declaring the scavenging to be disruptive to the ecology of the area and that all such activities were to cease. We thought it was aimed more at the commercial enterprises that collected the bones for gift shops and such. Dinosaur bone jewellery and belt buckles were all the rage at one point. The government fenced off the areas and posted signs and established huts to control the entry and exit to the most prolific grounds most at danger for exploitation. Or so we thought."

Ellen moved up beside him, but her eyes were far away. "Then they brought the big equipment. The government pushed back the boundaries and began issuing passes permitting entry into the area. Everyone was turned away, including scientists, unless they had government-issued permission to access the area. Some of those we knew applied to the government and those who were accepted soon became closed-mouthed about what they were being asked to study. They were sworn to secrecy, and eventually they stopped associating with us at all. Trucks began to leave the area, full of no one knew what, but by the sheer number, we deduced they must be carrying away artifacts in the armoured ones and debris in the garbage scows. So we started following the trucks."

"The garbage trucks came here. The armoured trucks went to a secured warehouse near Melona. We never could get a look inside that one," said Albert.

Mitch scratched his ear, puzzled. "Why dig through this dump? I still don't understand."

"It's because, in all of this garbage, there may be a piece that they missed. A piece of a dinosaur so important to the government that they will kill to protect the secret," said Ellen.

"What secret?" said Mitch.

"The secret of the disease being unleashed by the government, on our unsuspecting world. We believe that they unearthed something deadly. Our bet is that it is the same disease that killed the dinosaurs in the first place. A plague that we cannot begin to stop until we find the root cause. That is why we dig."

Mitch sifted the concept through his mind. "OK, say that this is all true," he held up his hand when Albert opened his mouth in rebuttal, "and the disease issue that is affecting the land is related to the dinosaur bones. What do you expect to accomplish in the end?"

"Find a cure of course! We are trying to save this world! We gave up our family to do so."

"Yeah, well as to that, why didn't you just bring them with you?" He shook off the protest he knew was coming. "Never mind. What I really need to know is how does all of this tie in to the greenhouses? You know about them, right?"

"Yes. We are aware of the greenhouses," said Ellen. "We are not sure of their significance, but we have theories. We are waiting for the scientists of the SOS to tell us this, but they are working in many scattered locations. The SOS operates in small cells so that if a government raid were to happen, they would not grab all of us at once. But this makes it difficult to share information too. A courier must move our results from cell to cell as we don't dare trust the Internet, where it is even available. The government monitors every transmission from every server. Rogue servers that are not registered are shut down within days. There is no such thing as 'freedom of information' any longer. Only the rich can afford Internet service, so it makes it super easy to know who is using it and for what purpose. Cell phone service collapsed long ago, as you know. So most of the SOS teams have gone back to a shortwave system of radio and encoded broadcasts. You can only send a limited amount of information that way, however, and a lot of what we are dealing with are samples and data slides. It must be transported. SOS couriers run between sites, sharing the results of their research. The cell you see here," she waved a hand back at the trestle, "is one of many."

"So you are searching for dinosaur bones too small to be caught in the machinery the government was using, to study the same thing they were? How do you know what it was? How do you even know it is related to dinosaur bones? They could have been searching for anything."

"We know because we were two of the scientists that applied and were accepted into the government ranks. We were part of their secret order, initially." Albert grimaced, anger flashing across his face. "That is, until we discovered the truth. The government is behind the entire ecological disaster. Every last bit of it."

"I thought so, too," said Mitch, "but I have never had any evidence to back up my hunch. So what have you discovered? Why bring me here?"

"We knew you were searching for us and had been since we disappeared. We also hoped you could help us with a small snag we have run into. Come, let me show you." Albert crossed over to a small bridge spanning twin piles of refuse then took a staircase that led back down to ground level, taking the steps two at a time.

Mitch hurried to keep up. At the base of the stairs, a pair of glass doors on sensors came into view and shushed open, parting to allow them entry. It took a minute or so for his sight to adjust to the dim interior. When it did, what he saw took his breath away. Mitch whistled as he slowly he entered the cavern, his eyes roving over the incredible sight. Rows and rows of incubators stood solemn sentry, organized into groups, like peas in a pod. Lights blinked on the front of the pods, and a light in the ceiling brightened as he paused in front of a tube. Floor to ceiling in height, each pod contained a person. There was no defining factor to the arrangements that he could determine. Some pods contained women, some contained men. They were of different heights, differently dressed, and different ethnic groups. There were even a few children in the groups. Mitch couldn't stop his eyes from roving over the rows and rows of tubes.

"What is going on here? They are all in stasis, right?" asked Mitch, his eyes studying a blond-haired boy of about twelve. His heart lurched. He reminded him of Alexa. "Are they infected?"

"They were all stung by bees. Each and every one of them," said Ellen.

Astonishment washed over Mitch. He ran a hand down his face, welcoming the feel of the scruff on his chin as his eyes took in all the people in stasis chambers.

"How in the world did you get them all here?"

"That is a fascinating story, for another time. Suffice it to say, if we had left them where we discovered them, they would be truly dead," said Albert, his voice gruff.

Mitch turned around to stare down the two scientists at his back. He folded his arms and his biceps bulged, as he tensed to do battle. "I am not leaving this spot until you explain why you kidnapped me and brought me here. Clearly you want something, *and I am not cooperating until you explain everything.* Are they victims of government experimentation? Or did you do this to them?"

The Gainsboroughs exchanged glances but remained silent.

"I have been caring for your children," he continued. "Did you know? For the last three months, I have been housing and feeding them, and all this time, you have been alive. How could you abandon them so? You made no provisions for their welfare at all. You left them to rot while you staged your own abduction by the government? Is that what I am to understand about all of this?"

"*No!*" shouted Ellen, angry tears sparkling in her eyes.

They were the same shape as Avalon's, Mitch noted with a distracted corner of his mind.

"We did not abandon them. We were taken, just as they told you. They dragged us away from our children to continue our work on these," she pointed at the closest tube, "popsicles and left our children to starve. There was nothing we could do. We were under lock and key at all times. We were not allowed any communication with the outside world."

"You created these catatonic people? This is your work? You have been the ones experimenting on people?" asked Mitch, his voice vibrating with fury.

"No. We did not create them. We were brought in to save them," said Albert.

Mitch's eyes travelled between the pair. "Explain," he said, his voice a flat slap.

Albert unclenched his fists, pacing the narrow confines of the space between the pods to ease the angry tension stiffening his shoulders. "The government is experimenting with a rare form of DNA that is found within a certain variety of dinosaur. Our research determined that the DNA of these dinosaurs had been altered by their exposure to a prehistoric version of today's carpenter bee. During our college forays into the badlands where dinosaur bone deposits are most plentiful, we happened on an area of fossilized remains that showed some of the bony processes of the dinosaurs had been hollowed out. A network of honeycomb-like complexes had replaced the internal structure of the bones. Fascinated, we took a large thigh bone back to our lab at the college for closer study. What we discovered there was exciting beyond belief. The dinosaurs had been hijacked by a clever species of bee that utilized their very bone structures to create a safe haven to protect them from the ravages of an environment so out of control that it was killing their hosts in droves. The theory we developed was that the bees would swarm a dinosaur and bore into their bony structures at the ridges of the back or of a horn and, once inside the relatively soft core, continue to bore until they reached a sheltered location. Hip bones and sockets were a favoured place to build their vast honeycombs. Living host or dead, it mattered not to the bees. Over many millennia the bees evolved, taking on some of the DNA characteristics of their hosts and were transformed."

Mitch frowned at the pair of them. "So? What is the point? What does any of this have to do with the government? Or with these people?" He gestured toward the silent host crowded around them.

Ellen took up the recounting of the story. Her face was pasty white in the dull light of the overhead bulbs. "Inside the dinosaur bones, we found living specimens. The honeycombs had protected them, keeping them in stasis within the cavities for all this time. We were able to reanimate them."

Mitch's frown faded into a scowl, and he suddenly had the urge to scratch all over. His skin crawled with apprehension, the same sensation he felt when he knew a showdown was about to happen, but it was a confrontation that could not be avoided. He tensed, his fight-or-flight instinct kicking in. *Bad news is coming, very bad news,* he thought.

"Don't you see? These people are infected the same way the dinosaurs are. The bees are growing inside them."

Mitch's chin dropped. "Growing inside them? But...there is only one bony structure big enough to house a bee colony. You mean, there are colonies of prehistoric bees buzzing around inside their heads?"

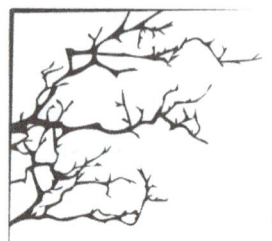

Chapter 5
The Secret Lair

Avalon crouched behind the bumper of the burnt-out car, behind Magnum's broad back. Her knife slid in and out of her sleeve as she chafed over not being able to see the threat ahead of them. On one hand was Magnum who, for all her taunting words, was as silent as a corpse when on patrol. Cris, on the other hand, was not. A low hiss sounded in Avalon's ear.

"Can't you crouch any smaller? Get your ass down and stay behind Magnum, or I will—"

"Or you will what?" interrupted Avalon, glaring over her shoulder at Cris. "I have lived longer on the street than not without the backup protections of the likes of her." She jammed her thumb in Magnum's direction.

"Shut up, both of you," growled Magnum in a low voice that barely carried back to them. "I spy four armed people out front of the building. They have knives. No guns that I can spot. One has a baseball bat stashed in the doorway of the cannery. See that fire escape there?" She pointed to the right of the doorway. "There is a fifth up top of the building acting as a look out."

Avalon leaned out around Magnum to have a look, and Cris hauled her back by the shoulder.

"Fire escape, roof, got it," said Cris, giving Avalon a murderous glare.

Avalon smirked at the look of annoyance on Cris's face. "There is a sixth person," she said, "there, in the shadow of the burnt-out bus."

Magnum's head turned in the direction of the bus and stared intently for several moments. "You're right. Good catch, Avalon. His coat is working as camouflage. I missed him." She considered the layout of the people, thinking. "Three against six. Not good odds. I wonder why they brought so many? The Imbroglio gang likes to operate in pairs. Less chance of a street fight breaking out."

"Hey, look over there," said Avalon. "At the side door by the bus. It's opening."

"Decoy," muttered Magnum. "They are all decoys."

"Yeah," said Cris, "and look at what's coming up the alley."

A black van slowly drove up the alley, making hardly a sound as it moved. Tinted windows blocked any view of the interior or the driver. The van pulled up just short of the street, and the driver and passenger doors opened. A man and a woman, dressed in black, stepped from the van, their hands tucked inside the pockets of their coats.

"Cops!" whispered Magnum.

Avalon watched the pair approach the burnt-out bus, and a chill raced down her spine. "No, it's worse. They are feds."

"Shit." Magnum pulled away from the edge, backing up into the pair. "Let's get out of here. We don't want their kind of attention." She grabbed Avalon's arm to turn her around, but Avalon shook it off with a scowl.

"I'm not going anywhere until I see what they are up to." She slipped past Magnum and took up the lead spot, crouching low.

The woman in black wore skin-tight leggings and high-topped black boots. Her eyes darted in all directions, clearly not trusting the sentries posted by the Imbroglio's. Her eyes settled on the spot where Avalon hid, and she froze, staring back at the woman.

"Don't move," she whispered, "she is staring right at us."

A sharp word from her male companion drew her attention away from their location, and she hurried to catch up to his retreating back. The crack widened in the doorway and they slipped inside, the door closing behind them. The Imbroglio lookout under the bus crawled out and started walking down the alley, searching the van's back trail.

"I'm going inside," said Avalon, as she sprang to her feet and sprinted off across the open space.

"Avalon! Shit!" swore Magnum. With a quick glance to check the location of the decoys, she ran after Avalon with Cris on her heels.

They caught up to her at the side of the burnt-out bus then followed her as she dashed into the tiny concealment of the doorframe. Avalon pressed her ear against the peeling paint of the wooden door, listened for signs of occupants on the other side, and then slowly turned the knob. It was unlocked. She eased the door open an inch, pausing to listen once again. No sound reached her ear. She pushed with her shoulder, and the door opened wide enough to allow them to slip inside. Then Cris closed it with a soft click.

High dirty windows filtered a murky light into the abandoned garage. Oily patches stained the rough concrete and empty oil change pits carved rectangular hazards across the floor. The room was otherwise empty. Magnum grabbed Avalon's injured arm and squeezed hard.

"Oww!" hissed Avalon, angry eyes sparking in her determined face.

"Let's get one thing straight," said Magnum, "I am in charge of this escapade."

"No one commands me. I answer only to myself. Besides, you have no idea what you are walking into here. I do. So if you are smart you will follow my lead. Now, let go of me." She stared down Magnum. After a moment's hesitation, she pushed Avalon away.

"Go ahead then. Get yourself killed. Just don't expect us to save you...again." Cris smirked and folded her arms, daring Avalon to go on alone.

Avalon shrugged and took off at a run, not caring if they followed. Anywhere there were feds, there was a lead to her parents and that was all she cared about. Everyone else could rot.

She flattened herself on the wall of a doorway that lead of the mechanical bay, inching forward until she could peer down the hallway. Several doors branched off of the dark space and from the far end, a light shone through a pane of glass covered over in old newspaper. A soft murmur reached her ears.

"Stay here!" she commanded. Without looking back to see if they had obeyed, Avalon slunk into the dark corridor. She flitted from grey haze to dim shadow, a determined shade on a quest to reveal all. At the door, she ducked low under the glass and pressed her ear to the crack of the frame. This time she heard the voices clearly.

"They have been this way for a week now. I see no change." The woman's voice echoed slightly as it rose in anger. "This is useless. They are dying like all the others."

"What does it matter? There are plenty of street rats round. No one misses the homeless when they disappear off the street. This is a convenient way to test the serum. If they die, they die. One less person to kill off later," the man said in a bored voice.

Heels clicked as one of the occupants of the room crossed the tile floor. "This one doesn't look as bad as the other two. Maybe she can handle another dose. Come look."

Shuffling sounds met Avalon's ear as Magnum crouched down beside her.

"Yeah. She looks healthier than the rest. Let's give her another dose of the serum." A metal clasp snapped back, pinging metal on metal. "There, in her other arm, this one looks like a drug addict on a bad run," said the man.

"All right, let's get out of here before someone spots our van."

Avalon grabbed Magnum's arm and pulled her into a side room, easing the door closed then huddled in the dark behind it. Footsteps sounded in the hallway and passed by their hiding spot. She hoped that Cris had been paying attention, otherwise the game was up. The footsteps continued on their way, and the exterior door opened and closed with a hollow boom. Avalon eased to her feet and then tiptoed to the door, peeking through the glass. The hallway was empty as far as her eye could see.

Magnum touched her shoulder and put her lips against Avalon's ear. "We need to get out of here before we get caught!" she whispered, her voice tight with anger.

"Not until I see what is in that room. You stay here. I won't be but a minute." She pulled open the first door, checked to make sure the coast was clear, then ran over to the newspapered door and pushed it open. Inside were a dozen hospital gurneys lined up in two rows of six, under the grimy windows set high in the walls. Only three were occupied, two on one side, one on the other. Together, they approached the closest of the gurneys and peered down at the person laying there. Both girls gasped out loud at the inhuman features that stared back at them. The face of the person who lay in the bed was swollen beyond recognition. His face was mass of large red welts so large that they obscured his eyes and mouth from view. The location of his mouth could be guessed at, only because of the orderly arrangement of the swellings, producing a puffy line where they assumed a mouth would exist. They assumed the person was human because of the lack of hair on his head. Avalon didn't care to check any further to confirm the theory. She shuddered to think what might lie below the filthy covers. His chest rose and fell, accompanied by shallow, irregular gasps as he struggled to breathe.

"What has happened to them"?" Magnum's tough exterior failed her in face of the torturous remains lying in the accompanying bed. "What have they done to these people?"

Avalon looked over at Magnum. Sweat had broken out on Magnum's face and her fist rose to her mouth to stop herself from throwing up. She didn't seem to notice that she had done it.

"This is what I needed to know," said Avalon. "The experiments being run on these people are the reason my parents were kidnapped and taken away. They knew this was going on. They were trying to stop it."

"What are they doing to them? They look like they have been swarmed by bees." Magnum stepped back from the bedside.

"Very good, Firebrand. So your crew has some brains after all."

The voice dropped in behind them like ice cubes down the backs of their shirts, chilling them to the bone. Avalon whipped around, knife in hand but her legs were kicked out from under her. She fell, striking her head against the metal bed frame. The room spun, and she slumped onto her side, stunned.

"Drop the knife, Firebrand, and you won't get hurt." The skinny Imbroglio boy waved a long-bladed knife in Magnum's direction, motioning with his hand to a second boy to move in closer. "Take her knife, Frank."

A shorter boy with a shock of red hair moved into the light of the window, approaching Magnum with caution.

Magnum's eyes flickered between her two opponents, brandishing her knife as they tried to cut her off.

Avalon moaned on the floor and the first Imbroglio lashed out with her foot, kicking Avalon in the face. Her eyebrow split, spilling blood down her face as she slumped to the floor. Furious, Magnum launched herself at the closest boy, a bull charging a red cape. They collapsed on the floor, wrestling, while Cris engaged the remaining kid, attacking with a swift series of kicks and punches that drove her opponent back. The sounds of grunts and thuds filled the air. Avalon slowly pushed herself to her feet, staggering sideways for several steps and breaking her fall by grabbing onto a plastic conduit attached to the wall behind the beds. The conduit buzzed under her hand. She blinked the blood out of her eyes to look at it closer but froze at the sound of a voice behind her.

"That's enough. Drop your knives. Now!"

The barked command echoed through the room, bringing everyone to a halt.

Avalon groaned. The two feds had returned and stood blocking the exit, their guns leveled. Magnum's combatant swung a final blow at Magnum, connecting his fist to her jaw. She crumpled to the floor, stunned.

"Enough, I said!" barked the male officer, and the boy confronting Cris smirked as he put his knife away.

Cris was still on her feet and ran over to help Magnum get up, slinging her slack arm around her shoulder. "Stand up, Magnum, shake it off," she whispered in her ear.

"Well, this is unfortunate for you three," said the female officer in a cold voice. "We were about to go searching for more test subjects, and here they walk in willingly! These three," she gestured toward a bed, "are pretty much used up. But while they lasted, they told us a lot, like how the bees are attracted to movement, how it increases their aggression. Like how certain colours excite them and others do not. They have a collective intelligence. Did you know that? In the past, we called it a 'hive mind' but it's much more than shared instinct. It is shared knowledge. They grow and adapt to their surroundings based on the knowledge they obtain, and these bees are acquiring knowledge at an alarming rate. You see, *they have assimilated the minds of these people.* Unfortunately, none of them were intelligent enough to help them in a significant fashion, but who knows? Maybe you three are smart enough to bring about the evolution we have been striving to accomplish."

Magnum and Cris's mouths opened in horror at her recitation.

"Enough talk," barked her companion. "You three, down on the floor."

For Avalon, it was old news. She edged closer to the joint of the pipe, her eyes pinned on the gun-wielding officers. She swayed with her head down, partly to give the impression of being stunned and weakened and partly to examine the pipe closer. She shivered at her mad, mad plan. The male officer gestured for them to come over to them. Cris pulled Magnum along beside her, and, after a few steps, Magnum shook off Cris's help. As they walked over, the two Imbroglios circled around behind them. Avalon watched them close the gap. When she judged they were only steps from the door, she pulled her hood up over her head and yelled.

"Magnum, Cris, *run*!" She threw her weight against the pipe. With a groan and a snap, the joint let go and Avalon ran for the door.

An angry, horrifying buzzing filled the air, as thousands of angry bees swarmed out of the end of the tube. The federal officers stood stock still for a moment in shock as the bees swarmed into a black cloud. Magnum and Cris threw themselves against the doors just as the two Imbroglio teens screamed and ran at the feds, stumbling into them and leading the angry bees directly to the two officers. They went down in a tangled mass, bees swarming the four screaming victims.

Avalon slowly moved along the wall working her way to the door-way where the door had swung mostly closed after the Firebrand teens near escape. At the last second, she could control her fear no longer and lunged for the open doorway, running through and slamming it shut behind her.

Gasping, Avalon lowered her hood. A piercing pain stabbed into her neck. On instinct, she swatted the bee, smashing it against the side of her neck. "Come on, we need to get out of here!"

They ran down the hall, across the garage, and through the doors without a care for who waited outside. It was blessedly empty. Fear giving their feet wings, they dashed down the closest alley.

Avalon blinked. Her vision was acting funny, clouding over then clearing, then clouding over again. She tripped and went down, skidding along the cobblestones to a halt. She tried to push up off the ground, but her vision narrowed. She caught a glimpse of Magnum and Cris turning around before her sight tunneled away and she faded into oblivion.

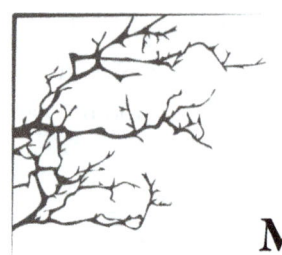

Chapter 6
Medical Records

ALEXA DRAGGED THE HEAVY briefcase to the easy chair within reach of Peet's hand. He gripped the handle and hauled it onto his lap, a groan escaping his lips as the stitches pulled, and then pushed on two metal buttons. The clasps released with dual snaps, and Peet lifted the lid of the bulging case. Inside were stacked over one hundred file folders, filled with sheaves of paper reports. The tab of each folder gave the name of a patient, their date of birth, and a hospital ID code. He picked up the first folder and flipped it open, thumbing through the loose pages. Peet's eyes scanned the contents while a long whistle of appreciation escaped his lips.

"This is quite the stash of information. Are the feds aware you have these?"

"No." Worry wrinkled Peet's winged brows. "At least, I don't think they do," said Dr. Song.

"It only takes one person to talk. How many people know about these records?" asked Peet.

"Myself, my secretary while I was still at the hospital, and my daughter," said Dr. Song.

"And every doctor who filled out a report?" asked Peet. "That is the problem."

"No, you don't understand. I filled out those reports, every single one of them."

Peet's mouth opened in surprise. "That is a ton of work. When did you find the time to examine every one of these patients?"

"I set up a control protocol under the guise of biohazard security. It required a secondary entry on all patients of interest to the government. I had to sign off on the electronic file and conducted my own review while I did so. Only my secretary, Sylvia, could interpret my notes. No one else could read my handwriting." Dr. Song smiled. "Sylvia died about a year ago. As far as I know, she took the secret with her to the grave."

"And your daughter?"

"She is part of the SOS initiative. SOS stands for—"

"Seeds of Survival," Peet finished the sentence. "Is it safe to assume that you are in contact with the SOS, then?" Dr. Song nodded agreement. "Then why have you not passed this research on to them? Surely they could use the information?"

"Ah, well you see, I have been in radio contact with them, but not physical. I am a modern homing pigeon, only I don't go anywhere. The signals come to me."

Peet frowned. "Does the SOS know you have the files?"

"Yes, but I don't think they know how many."

Peet picked up the first file, flipped it open again and began to read. The subject was female. Everything was there, from first admittance, tests run and results, daily observations and interventions, and eventually the date and time of death. Peet examined the two dates. Three days. She had died within three days of presenting herself at the hospital with symptoms of a deep chest congestion and disorientation. Peet picked up a print from an MRI film examining the results. What he saw made bile rise in his throat. A good portion of her brain was missing. But that wasn't what alarmed him. It was what had replaced the missing tissue. A symmetrical web-like structure was clearly visible, occupying the left half of her frontal lobe. Disbelieving his eyes, Peet said "Is that...*a honeycomb?*"

"Yes. Hard to believe, isn't it? And there are ninety-nine more cases just like it in the folders below that one"." Dr. Song pointed at the open case on Peet's lap. "Every single one of those cases were treated by the same two doctors, sent over by the government, and assigned specifically to this phenomenon. It was like they knew the sick would start arriving at our doors."

"How so?"

"Those two doctors arrived within hours of the first cases staggering in through the emergency room doors. They virtually commandeered the old psychiatric wing, citing war time ordinances and waving signed documents from the feds. They came with an armed accompaniment, too. A sniper team in fatigues. We just moved aside and let them do their thing. They rounded up the ill with certain symptoms and herded them down the hall to the empty psych wing, shouting orders for supplies and commandeering staff to gather it."

Peet stared in amazement at Dr. Song. "Who were these doctors? Did you recognize them?"

Dr. Song's eyes flickered to Alexa then back to Peet. "Yes. It was a pair of young, up and coming disease prevention doctors from the university. Doctor and Doctor Gainsborough."

Alexa's eyes widened. "Mama? Papa?"

Dr. Song nodded. "Yes, it was them. Whether they were working voluntarily or were being forced, we did not know. We were never allowed to speak to them directly, or alone. Later, they showed up at the SOS. From what I have heard, it was an interesting conversation that went down."

Peet flipped through a few more files, frowning. "Did every patient die?"

"Yes. There was nothing we could do for them."

"And what about those we saw at the hospital crowding the corridors? Are they all infected too?"

Dr. Song shook his head. "No, those are just regular illnesses, if there is a such a thing anymore. Most of them are suffering from starvation and dehydration. But those one hundred cases in front of you on your lap? They were in unprotected contact with the pathogen, and by contact, I mean they were purposely exposed."

"You don't think this was an accident?" Peet's voice was sharpened as the reality Dr. Song's words sank into his mind. "You think they were being experimented on? That is a pretty massive accusation, Doctor."

Dr. Song's eyes narrowed in appreciation of Peet's unwillingness to accept his words on face value. "Indeed, they are. But you see, we found more."

"More what?" Alexa edged closer to Peet's chair. "You found mummies? Zombies?" She shuddered, her imagination running wild.

Dr. Song smiled at her words, then it faded away. "No, Alexa, no zombies. Zombies make for great stories, but it really isn't possible to animate the dead." His gaze rose to meet Peet's troubled eyes. "We found one of their experimental stations. They have them scattered all over the city. What we discovered was that the walking wounded who showed up at the hospital had escaped one of these 'experimental hospitals' for lack of a better term. These mini-prisons are set up in abandoned sectors of the city, and the subjects drawn in to them are the homeless, people who no one will miss. Lured with the promise of food and a warm bed, they willingly agree to whatever they want, but they never leave. We found one such facility and carried away the people there. It is part of the work being done by the SOS."

Dr. Song's hand brushed the top of Alexa's hair. "Your parents," he said softly, "are two of the scientists working to undo the damage to these people."

"What is wrong with them?" she asked, her eyes wide.

"They have been stung. At first, we thought it was just a remnant of some colony of killer bees, but these are worse, much worse. They take their natural aggression to a whole new level. We think they have been altered somehow."

Peet let out a low whistle, as understanding dawned in his eyes. "A super bee," he muttered.

"Yes. A super bee experiment that has gone horribly wrong. That is what we suspect, too."

Peet shifted, wincing. "Damn, why did I have to get shot now? I don't have time for this crap."

"You will heal faster if you don't move around so much. Give it a week at least before you attempt to do any serious activity. You should be able to get around then, without bleeding at least."

"I need to find Mitch. He needs to know about this. Perhaps he can pull some strings at the police station."

"Who is Mitch?"

Alexa piped up, pleased to contribute. "He is the cop that arrested my sister, Avalon, for stealing then broke her out of jail to come get me."

Dr. Song stared at Alexa, the beginning of a smile twitching in the corner of his mouth.

"Another rebel. I should have guessed." He shuffled over to Peet's side and drew aside his borrowed bathrobe to check on the dressing over his leg wound. "You know, if this had been left any longer, you would have died. The bullet hit the femoral artery of your thigh. Sit still and rest. I will see if I can raise the police station via the shortwave. But understand, I am not going to tell them where I am or where to find us. Now, what message do you want me to pass on?"

Peet picked up a scratch pad of paper and a pen. The first page contained a short grocery list. He flipped it over and tore out the page underneath and scrawled a short message. It said "Careful with package. Highly contagious. Use extreme caution or we will all need an SOS." He handed it to the doctor then motioned for Alexa to help him stand.

He lurched to his feet then hobbled back over to the couch, sinking down with a grateful sigh. "I need to rest."

Alexa tucked the blankets around him and tiptoed out of the room following Dr. Song back to the shortwave set to send their precious message.

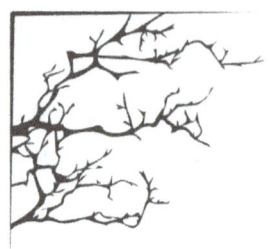

Chapter 7
Rabbits

DR. SONG TWIDDLED WITH the dials on the shortwave, fine tuning the signal until it was so thin that only someone specifically listening on that frequency would be able to find it. Still, caution dictated that he disguise the message as much as possible to confuse anyone who might stumble across the transmission.

"Brier Rabbit to Snowshoe Hare. Brier Rabbit to Snowshoe Hare. Are your ears pointed?"

Static filled the room. He repeated the message and on his third call, the shortwave cracked. "Snowshoe Hare. How's the weather?"

"Storm is brewing. Hot and dry as a desert yet clouds are gathering. Got us a sick buck here. Kit is fine, hopping about, checking on the grazing. Buck ran into a hedgehog. Was bitten but on the mend. They pop up everywhere nowadays."

"Same here," said Snowshoe." "We found us a buck too, one with very long teeth. He talks a lot, too. He brings a storm with him I think. Time to send him back to his den and see if he can sort through the weather signals. With a little luck, maybe he can turn the storm around. Has connections to the weather gods, I think."

"Does the hare have a name?"

Static fed along the signal for a moment then cleared. "He says he is called Hotshot. Never heard of a rabbit called Hotshot. Hotshot Hare it is."

"Well, you tell Hotshot to watch for rogue rabbits when he gets back. Some are working for the processing plant. Unless he wants to end up on someone's dinner plate, he had better lie low. There is one doe there in the main den that might be of help."

"He has heard your words. He will be nosing around starting tomorrow. We will let him know how to recognize your den," said Snowshoe. "Hotshot wants to know if anyone has heard from the rogue doe. The one that went to find the Jack Rabbit lair."

Dr. Song looked to Peet, who shook his head. "No one here has heard from her. I think our buck here wants to go after her."

"We think she has been gone long enough now. Time to bring her back home," said Snowshoe.

"Tell Hotshot that his parcel is buzzing with potential. It is even more dangerous than he realizes," said Brier.

"We have brought Hotshot up to speed. He knows the risks."

"Excellent. Tell him to meet up with his old den mates in two weeks' time. Our buck should have mended from the hedgehog bite by then."

"Understood. A new thistle was discovered, we are sending you one too in the next litter. Over and out."

The line went dead, and Dr. Song sat back.

Alexa giggled. "You are Brier Rabbit?"

Dr. Song smiled down at the child's happy face and nodded. "And Snowshoe is someone you know, I think."

"Really? How would I know them?"

"I believe he may be your father."

The smile slid from Alexa's face. "My father is dead." All trace of humour was gone.

"Your father is missing," corrected Dr. Song. "There is a big difference."

Alexa slid off the chair she had been perched on to watch Dr. Song operate the radio. "It doesn't matter. I hardly remember them anymore. Avalon is the only family I have." She walked out of the room.

Dr. Song idly spun the dials on the shortwave, thinking. *I could get them back together, Alexa and her parents. It could be arranged.* But the Gainsboroughs had left specific instructions to the SOS that under no circumstances were they to expose the Gainsborough children to the disease. Dr. Song no longer believed that was possible to keep them safe merely by distancing them from their parents. *They may very well be safer closer to their parents, but their parents are working on the disease.*

The disease was spreading at an alarming rate. It made the work they were doing that much more vital. If an antidote could not be found in time, their world was doomed, as was every human within it. The toll of the failing ecological systems was being felt in every corner of the world. Already they were dependent on imports from areas away from the epicenter of Solace and Melona.

A heavy sigh escaped Dr. Song's lips as he pushed up from his chair. He shuffled out of the radio room and back to where Peet sat, bending and straightening his leg, testing how the torn muscles of his thigh were healing. He winced and grimaced, but his lips were clamped shut and he made no sound. Dr. Song took Peet's leg and bent it at the knee then pressed his thigh to his chest then pulled it straight again. With this movement, a faint groan escaped Peet's lips.

"Still tender with deep flexion, eh? Come, stand up." He offered Peet his arm to steady him. "Let's take a short walk around the outside of the house." He placed Peet's shoes in front of his feet, and Peet shoved them in, leaving the laces loose.

"I could use some fresh air." Together they stumbled out the door.

ALEXA WATCHED THE PAIR stumble out the front door. As soon as it closed behind them, Alexa scurried into the radio room. She had been watching Dr. Song operate the wireless unit and was confident she knew how to do it. She flipped the power switch and then spun the tuning dial until she found the exact frequency she wanted, one she had memorized by heart. The unit glowed green, indicating the unit was ready to transmit. Alexa took a deep breath then picked up the hand-held mic and pushed the button on its stem.

"Alex...I mean Alice in Wonderland to Nivens. Come in please."

The shortwave crackled and hummed.

"Alice in Wonderland to Nivens. Come in, White Rabbit."

Silence.

"Alice in Wonder—" The radio receiver flashed and the voice of a young man reached her ears.

"White Rabbit is down a rabbit hole. This is March Hare."

Alexa peeked out the window. Dr. Song and Peet were just rounding the corner of the garage. "March Hare. I need to visit the last rabbit hole that Nivens and I went to together. There are some special carrots there that are needed for a friend. Could you have Nivens meet me at the entrance to the hole in two days' time? This is the hole underneath the lavender patch."

"Understood, Alice. We will send some other rabbits along to help you forage. By the way, a rabbit close to you has been found in the next den over. She was found in one of our rabbit holes but ran away. We think she may be sick. She ran into some hunters."

Alexa's pulse raced with alarm. "Is she OK? She is a reckless rabbit. Always sniffing at traps."

"We don't know. We are trying to find out. She is running with the wrong colony. There are many predators running wild in the forest nowadays. But the hunters are the worst. We avoid them as much as possible. They are snatching rabbits right off the runs. We are doing our best to learn their plans."

"Understood. I will meet up with Nivens at this hour tomorrow. Over and out."

Alexa turned off the wireless and put the chair back the way it was. She ran out of the room and to the kitchen, where a window displayed a view of the rear of the house. Peet and Dr. Song had just passed by and were almost to the third corner. Alexa grabbed a bag from under the sink and began shoving food into it, then ran back to her room and shoved it into the top of her backpack with all her belongings. She shoved it back under the bed and then went back to the living room, just as the door was opening. She held it wide while Peet limped into the room. His face was ashen, and he looked like he was about to throw up. He limped over to the couch and sank down into it, his eyes closing with exhaustion. Dr. Song lifted the injured leg, dragging a groan from Peet. He rolled up the pant leg and examined the area of stitches. They had torn and a fluid seeped from where the skin was supposed to have healed. The area around the bullet hole was red, the tissue inflamed.

"Damn!" The curse was incongruous, coming from the squat doctor. "It's infected! I'm sorry, Peet, but I don't have any more antibiotics. We need to bathe and clean this once again. You were too long without treatment, and the infection was already present by the time I got to you. Alexa, fetch my medical bag, please."

The door slammed shut behind Alexa as she ran to get the medical supplies. She knew it was low on all the necessary supplies. She had been watching the doctor treat Peet for a week now. It was why she had to go. She knew of a stash of medical supplies. If Peet was going to recover, she needed to bring some back to the doctor. No one else seemed to be supplying him with any. She rushed back into the room and watched as Dr. Song pulled out the last of his antiseptic cream and some clean bandages.

"Warm water, Alexa, and in the cupboard beside the sink, there is a jar that is labeled 'Beeswax Ointment.' Bring that, also, please."

Alexa did as she was bidden, returning with the bucket of water and a clean washcloth, the jar of ointment tucked under one arm.

Dr. Song began to wash the wound once again as she watched. She had the routine down now and handed Dr. Song the items he needed before he asked. As she went about the chore mechanically, her resolve firmed. She would gather the supplies Dr. Song needed and make contact with her friend at the same time. It was time for her to join the fight and do something. *I may be twelve, but I am no longer a child*, she thought.

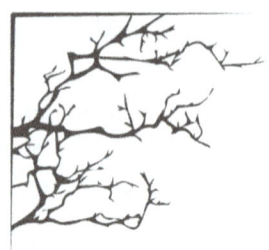

Chapter 8
Accusations

PAM WALKED THROUGH the encampment, waving in response to the called greetings. Her wave may have been relaxed, but her steps were not. She had a bone to pick with the chief.

Pam had returned to her camp to find Mitch's Mustang still parked where he had left it. He had never returned but disappeared mid-trip somehow. Outwardly, she was calm, but inside anger bubbled under the surface like a capped volcano, ready to explode with the pressure.

Betrayed by my own clan, my own family was her furious thought, her stomach churning with anger.

The chief's tent was guarded by the usual contingent of warriors, who did not stop her as she pushed aside the entrance flaps. As she straightened, she found the chief standing beside a small table, pouring himself a cup of fragrant tea. He turned as she entered and a smile of greeting passed over his face.

"Pam, would you like some tea?" He proffered his cup, which Pam took from him while he poured a second.

"I am going to guess you are not here for a social visit. Your face would do well on a totem." He walked over to a chair flanking the cold firepit and waited for her to sit down beside him. "Now, what is your problem, Pamissa?"

His use of her pet name only irritated Pam further. "You know perfectly well why I am here. Where is Mitch? You promised him safe passage!"

"And he is perfectly safe, I assure you. Why do you doubt this?"

"His car is still sitting by my temporary camp, that's why! Where is he?"

"His presence was requested by the SOS. They wanted to talk to him. I do not know where he is specifically. But they would not harm him. They need him. I had warriors escort him to the rendezvous point." He took a sip of tea.

Pam waited for him to continue. When he did not speak again, she prompted "Well? When is he coming back?"

"I do not know."

"Where is he being returned?"

"I don't know that, either."

"You don't know. You handed him off to complete strangers, and you don't even know if he is being returned? What if they are not who you think they are? What if they mean to do him harm?" Pam's face flushed with anger.

The chief studied the woman before him then sighed. "We know he is safe because the ones who took him are in charge of the caverns. They come on a regular basis."

"Then maybe you can explain this?" Pam held up a bloodied cloth. It was a piece of Mitch's shirt. She was sure of it. "Why would he need to be beat up, to be taken to meet with allies?"

The chieftain frowned at the offending cloth. "You are sure it belongs to him?"

Pam nodded.

"I do not know how to answer you, Pam."

He got up from his chair and stalked to the door to speak to the sentries then returned. He sat back down and waited. Several minutes passed and then the flap opened and a pair of young men entered. Spying Pam sitting in the chair opposite their chief, their gait slowed. The chieftain stood and went to sit in his chair of authority then motioned for the warriors to approach him. Pam got up and joined the warriors, standing by their side.

"This woman, your tribal sister, brings a complaint of abuse to the judgment chair. You have been accused of abusing her kin during a recent assignment." He turned to Pam. "Present your evidence."

"I found this bloody piece of my brother's clothing lying out front of the caves. I became concerned when he had not returned to his car as he intended to do after leaving the compound." Pam winced at her flimsy argument.

"You find a bit of soiled clothing, and you automatically believe he has been abused?" The taller warrior threw back his head and laughed. "A city dweller, out in the wilderness hurts himself and you immediately blame your adopted kin?" The laughter fell from his face, and he scowled at Pam. "I am offended at this accusation. What other proof do you have?" He folded his arms and glared at Pam.

The chieftain gazed back at Pam, waiting for her response. Instead, she took the attack.

"You deny escorting him to meet with the strangers who demanded his presence?"

"We do not deny it."

"Then what happened?"

"He fell. City men are soft. They are not used to our rough ways of travel. No doubt he was exhausted from his earlier travels. He hurt himself, but as you can see, it did not stop him from accompanying us. We delivered him to his plane and returned."

"Plane? On the flats?"

"Yes. You can fetch him yourself if you wish. He is due back later today."

Pam studied the faces of the two warriors. Their expressions gave nothing away. Stone-faced and stoic, they stared her down. Pam sensed a dare in their advice.

"Fine, I will meet him then and save you the bother. I am sure he will have a lot to say, and none of it meant for your ears."

They stared back at her, their faces impassive.

"Then it is decided," said the chieftain. "Leave us." His eyes followed the warriors as they left the tent. "Those two have been known to be rough on prisoners. Mitch was not a prisoner, however."

"What if they thought he was? What would they have done, in that case?"

"They are not restricted. They may handle a prisoner with whatever force is deemed necessary. Up to and including lethal if needed."

Pam shivered. "I will be on my way then. I want to be there when the plane lands. Do they still run on the same schedule?"

"Yes," said the chieftain.

"Then I will be going. Thank you for hearing me out. He has been hurt. I know it. Whether provoked or for some other reason, I will find out." She bowed to the chief and left the chambers.

Pam had left her motorbike at the edge of the village and hurried back to it now, anxious to reach the landing strip before the plane landed. She checked the height of the sun in the sky. Three hours till sunset, she judged. The plane usually came in about an hour before dark. She had plenty of time to arrive at the landing strip before Mitch. She climbed onto the bike and kicked it awake, and spun away from the village, revving the throttle. She vanished into a cloud of dust of her own making, the sound of the bike fading into the distance.

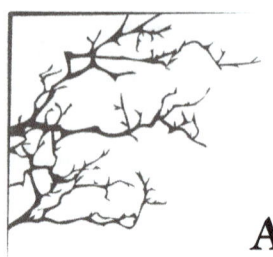

Chapter 9
Avalon's Struggle

AVALON' EYES FLUTTERED open. The light from the bare overhead bulb was swinging crazily, as though an earthquake was occurring, yet she felt no tremors. She blinked, trying to steady her vision, but it had the opposite effect. The only escape was in closing her eyes and still the world spun.

"Ahhhh!" groaned Avalon. She rolled onto her side and threw up. Or she tried to, but nothing came out.

"Hey, easy there," said a male voice, and a hand stroked her back.

"Trench?" she croaked, licking dry lips.

"Yeah, it's me Avalon. Go easy. You are very sick."

Avalon tried to swallow and found that she couldn't. Her throat was swollen shut. She gasped, drawing in a deep breath that caught on the obstruction. The sensation of choking on air made her eyes open again. Panic crawled on her skin, and she gasped and tried to sit up. Her arms flailed and her glazed eyes bulged. Trench grabbed her arms and pushed her back down.

"She is hyperventilating around the tube. Give me a syringe, quick!" he snapped, holding the struggling Avalon down against the sheets.

Cris handed Trench a needle brimming with sedative, and he plunged it into her upper arm. Avalon's struggles weakened, and then her tensed muscles relaxed. Her breathing eased along with it, allowing air to reach her lungs. Trench watched her sink back into unconsciousness, worry drawing a deep sigh from him.

"She can't keep going like this. She isn't able to eat." Magnum moved up on the other side of Avalon, gazing down at the unconscious teen. "She is a wreck. Look at the welts. They nearly cover her entire body. Her skin is expanding like a balloon."

"I know! I don't know what else to do for her." Trench had ventilated Avalon with a rough tube that they used in the kitchen. It was a crude effort, and one that he had only known because of his time at medical school. He had left Solace University when the economy collapsed. He had not been able to gather the required funds to continue. The middle-class kids had been the first to drop out. His knowledge of how to perform the procedure came as a result of his time spent assisting his veterinarian father. His father's practice had collapsed about the same time that he left school. When people were starving, they didn't take their pets to see a vet when a bullet was cheap. What he had been able to do for Avalon was keeping her temporarily alive, but she needed real help. "Were you able to get anyone from the SOS on the radio? Avalon needs a real doctor."

Magnum shook her head. "No. No one is answering right now. I will keep trying, but you know it's just chance when we do make contact."

"Keep trying. It's urgent. Broadcast twenty-four hours a day. We must reach them!"

"I will keep trying. I promise." Magnum touched his shoulder in comfort then left the room.

"Stay with her, Cris. I need to check on something."

Cris took his place beside Avalon as he got up and left the room. They had placed her back in the small office off of the kitchen. Two chairs had been brought in to sit beside Avalon's bed.

Trench crossed the kitchen to a small refrigerator, the only one that still worked in the restaurant. He opened the door, checking their scavenged supplies. They were running low on the medications they had stockpiled. He frowned, knowing a mission to restock them would be fraught with danger as it would pit them against the Imbroglio gang. They had been expanding their territory lately with the help of outsiders. Cris and Magnum's description of their encounter left no doubt as to who those outsiders were. If they had been recruited by the feds, then *the war* was about to escalate to new levels. He used the term subconsciously, for the Imbroglio gang used WAR as their symbol to define their territory. It was a turf war that encompassed the entire city. The main medical stash that they had located was in an abandoned veterinary clinic, on a hotly disputed border that the Imbroglio gang was sure to be patrolling. The takeover of the warehouse was ill news at the best of times, but now it weighed on Trench's mind.

He searched through the contents of the fridge, sorting the supplies and counting out what remained. They had gone through a lot of supplies since Avalon's arrival. He grimaced at the direction of his thoughts. Anyone else he would have tossed out of the gang, immediately. Everyone had to pull their own weight. It was part of the code. No one could be a drain to the others, or a burden.

Maybe I should toss her out. She has lived on her own long enough and survived. She doesn't need our protection. Yet there was something about her that attracted him as no other female had ever done. She was feisty and independent yet beneath that louder than life exterior, he sensed a kind person, one not jaded to life as they had become in the ghetto. That raw innocence that ran just below the surface attracted him in a way that shocked him. He knew he would not cast her out.

Trench ran a hand over his face when he realized he was standing in the fridge door opening, staring at nothing. Angry he went to close the door when a flash of movement caught his eye. Frowning, he opened the door wider and peered at the glass jar in the door tray. It was the jar that Cris and Magnum had put the squashed bee in after it fell from Avalon's clothing.

The bee was twitching. Trench leaned in closer and squinted at the bee. Its legs were jerking. He picked up the jar and held it up to the naked light bulb hanging from the ceiling. The second that the jar came in contact with the warmth and light from the bulb, the bee rolled onto its feet and began moving its wings. Shocked, Mitch watched as the torn wing regrew before his eyes. His eyes widened, and he hastily checked that the lid was on tight, then shoved it back in the refrigerator door and slammed it shut.

That damn bee was dead! I saw it! What the hell is it doing reanimating itself? He backed away from the fridge, eyes fixed on the container that suddenly seemed inadequate protection against what was re-growing in the jar. His first instinct was to flush it down a toilet, but would that be enough to destroy it? He doubted it.

Trench wrenched his eyes away from the fridge and ran over to a metal drawer that held odd supplies. He yanked it open and pulled a roll of duct tape from the drawer and was half way back to the fridge, intent on taping the jar shut when he realized all the medical supplies were in there. His anxious steps slowed then stopped, halfway back, considering the dilemma. He reversed his steps and pulled a piece of paper and a black marker of the same drawer, and wrote a warning in big, bold letters:

"*Bee is alive.* Do not open door unless absolutely necessary. *Trench.*"

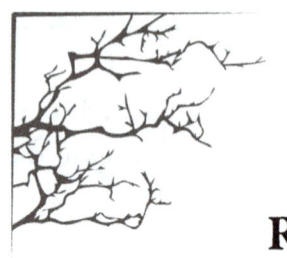

Chapter 10
Rogue Warriors

THE PLANE LANDED WITH a bump and coasted to a stop as the pilot cut the engines. Mitch unlocked his door and pushed it open, jumping to the ground. The Gainsboroughs followed him out of the plane. They walked a short distance away, not bothering to talk until the props stilled. Mitch caught a flash of movement at the far end of the landing strip and squinted into the setting sun, trying to determine who approached. The roar of the motorbike engine gave him an inkling of who it might be, but recent events had made him leery. The Gainsboroughs didn't hesitate, pulling twin revolvers and levelling them at the approaching rider.

"Wait! Stop!" Mitch jumped between the gun-wielding couple and the oncoming bike. "It's my sister, Pam." He waved his hands through the air at the Gainsboroughs then turned to face the bike.

Pam's frizzy grey hair flew in all directions as it was tossed about by the hot breeze created by the bike's speed.

"Pam, slow down!" he hollered, knowing it to be useless.

She could not possibly hear him over the roar of the engine, but the bike slowed anyway, sliding to a halt several feet away. Pam set the bike on its kick then stood up. She pulled off her helmet as she swung a leg off the bike and then walked over to them.

"It's my sister, Pam," Mitch said again to the tense couple over his shoulder.

Pam walked up Mitch and flung her arms around his waist, hugging him. He hugged her back then turned to present his sister.

However, the Gainsboroughs had turned around and were walking away.

"Wait!" called Mitch, but they ignored his request and climbed back into the Cessna. The engines roared to life. The plane taxied down the flat field gathering speed and then lifted into the sky.

"Well, that was weird," said Mitch, absently running a hand along his scruffy cheek as he watched the plane disappear from view.

"Yeah, that is the Gainsboroughs. They never stick around to talk. Always secretive, they are."

"How did you know it was them? They were walking away before you got to me." Mitch put his arm around Pam's shoulders, winced, and then lowered it.

Pam frowned at him, noting the bruising on his jaw beneath the burgeoning beard. "They keep to themselves. It's all business, cloak and dagger. I have never met them face to face. They never meet anyone face to face. You seem to be the exception to the rule. What happened, Mitch?"

Mitch's eyes swept the perimeter of their location, anxiety returning as he remembered his delivery to this spot a day earlier. "I was taken by some of the local thugs, roughed up, and deposited here for the Gainsboroughs. I got the impression that they didn't mean for it to go this far. I think their instructions were to bring me along quietly. Your new kin took it to mean silence me. At least, I hope that is all it meant." His eyes searched the lengthening shadows. "I'd really like to get somewhere safe before nightfall. I assume you have a camp set up nearby?"

"Yes, just over the rise. Come on."

Pam led Mitch back to the bike. A short ride later, she pulled into her makeshift camp strung between two scrubby pines. A cleft of rock sheltered them from the worst of the wind. Despite the persistent drought and the heat of day, temperatures dropped at night and with it a dampness that hinted that all moisture was not completely extinct in the soil.

Mitch grabbed Pam's flint from her pack and struck sparks into the kindling she had set within the circle of stones. The dry tinder caught almost at once, licking into flame and he added some smaller sticks. In short order, he had a cozy fire going. Pam brought her kettle and cooking grill and placed it over the fire, squeezing two cups worth of water from the water bag into the kettle and adding some leaves for tea. She tossed Mitch a package of dried foods, camp provisions that could travel everywhere. Jerky and nuts and disks of a flat, wild grain bread, all provided courtesy of the Seiko tribe. Mitch didn't bother to ask what kind of dried meat it was as he took hold of the end of it with his teeth and pulled. Sometimes it was better to not know. He chewed the tough jerky.

"Why does everything taste like chicken when you don't know what it is?"

Pam smiled and took a bite of her own then poured him some tea and handed him the cup. He sipped it gratefully, staring into the fire. She shifted a bundle by her side, and Mitch caught the gleam of a shotgun barrel. Seeing the interest in his eyes, she smiled. She handed him his duffel bag.

"I found that outside of the bunker. It was what had alerted me to your disappearance. You should find all your possessions intact."

Mitch opened the pack and right on top was his handgun. He grinned back at Pam and palmed the weapon into his hand, wrapped in a towel. He laid it across his lap, dropping the gun between his crossed legs. His eyes wandered back to the firepit.

"So, do you want to tell me about your adventure?"

Mitch pulled his eyes from the mesmerizing dance of flames then looked at Pam. Then in a low voice, he relayed all that had transpired.

She listened intently without interruption. At the end of his recitation, he fell silent. Pam said nothing. Eventually, she sighed and shifted to lie down beside the fire.

"I think we had better get some rest, Mitch."

"OK. I will take first watch. You sleep. I will wake you in four hours." Pam nodded and closed her eyes.

Mitch listened to the rustles of the night, marking the normal nocturnal sounds and listening for anything that sounded out of place. All was still, yet he couldn't help feeling like they were being observed. Something or someone was watching them. He was sure of it. His senses attuned to his surroundings, he picked up a piece of dried wood and pulled a jack knife from his pocket. He whittled to the flickering light. The piece of wood slimmed down, the pile of shavings at his feet perfect kindling for the morning. The piece of wood took the shape of a bird. As he carved the head, he realized it wasn't a bird but a bat. He was focused on the eyes, carving the small orbs when he heard a twig snap behind him.

Without thinking, he dropped to one knee and spun, throwing his knife. A blade whistled over his head and sailed harmlessly into the night, having missed its intended target, but his knife flew true and embedded itself in the chest of a young warrior. The man's eyes widened in surprise, and then he fell to the ground without a twitch.

Mitch barely spared him a glance as he yelled, "Pam!" Then, a warrior soaring through the air took him to the ground. He plowed Mitch into the dirt, and they rolled, just missing the firepit, the warrior coming out on top of Mitch. Another knife blade flashed, this one descending at his throat. Mitch blocked the stab with his arm, and the knife sliced into his sleeve. Mitch swore and bucked, throwing the warrior to the side. The sound of a shotgun sliding into firing position froze them both. Pam stepped into the firelight and held the shotgun aimed in the direction of the pair.

"I would suggest you both stop fighting, or you will both end up with britches full of bird shot. Mind you," she said, shifting the shotgun onto the warrior, "a face full of this will blind, maim, and most likely kill you as it rips your eyes and throat open. Go ahead. Move one more time." She brought the gun to aiming position. The warrior froze. "Drop the knife." The wicked switchblade landed in the dirt at Mitch's side. "Sit!" she commanded, indicating the log that Mitch had recently vacated.

Mitch unbuckled his belt and pulled it through his belt loops. He yanked the warrior's hands around behind his back and wound the belt around his wrists, pulling it painfully tight and buckling it into place. He shoved the warrior down to sit on the log.

"Mitch, check to make sure these are the only two." Pam kept her gun trained on the warrior.

Mitch grabbed his handgun and a length of rope from his pack and disappeared into the dark. He returned about twenty minutes later. "There might be three. I found their camp back by the airstrip. Two blankets but three packs." Mitch settled beside the fire, squatting to stir the coals. He dropped a few more sticks onto the glowing pile. "We will know if there is a third, the minute he approaches the camp." Mitch stood and walked over to still man. He checked the dead warrior on the ground. A search of the man revealed he had no pockets. There was nothing to identify him. "Who is he?" Mitch said as he straightened, addressing the man on the log. The warrior stared at him and sneered but did not speak. "Do you know who he is, Pam?"

Pam glanced at the corpse then back at her prisoner. "Yes, he is called Saecar. That one is Dromid," she said with a jerk of her head at the mum warrior. "If there is a third, then it is most likely Lippac. She is never found far from these two. They are trouble. Or at least they were," she said with a grim smile.

As though summoned by her words a female voice yelled, the sound flashing through their camp. Mitch grinned and got to his feet.

"That would be Lippac. I will go release her from the snare." Mitch pulled his handgun and disappeared into the shadows.

He did not go far, for his trap had been set on the main path in to their shelter. Curses filtered back into the camp and a thud, then the bushes shook. A few minutes later, a short, wiry woman limped into the clearing. Mitch had bound her hands and was leading her by a fist tangled in her hair and a knife pressed to her throat. A long scratch down her cheek welled with blood, but she paid it no heed. Mitch pushed her down onto Pam's log and stood over the woman.

"So, Saecar and Lippac. Why does this not surprise me? You always did resent my inclusion into the tribe."

Lippac spat in the dirt. "You are no Seiko."

Pam's hard gaze was met by angry eyes. "And you shame the Seiko. What did you intend to prove by harming my brother? He is here to help the Seiko, yet you attacked him. Why?"

Lippac's eyes flicked to her brother, then over at her dead boyfriend. A trace of sadness flashed then was pushed away. "You bring death to us all. You carry the plague into our tribe without regard for your 'family.' You take advantage of our people. Someone must stop you."

"Is that what you think? That I am exposing your people? We are all people! It doesn't matter the colour of our skin. Look at me," Pam barked when Lippac sneered and looked away. "Do you think the bees will stop at the border of your lands by magic? That they can read the totem markers and will be turned away? Even if the ancestors do intervene, the bees are not natural. They will not heed the ancestors any more than they heed us. We will all die if we do not work together."

Saecar finally spoke, breaking his stoic silence. "The bees do not harm us." The simple sentence hung in the air like a thunderclap. Heads turned toward him.

"What do you mean by that?" Mitch asked, his jaw dropping open.

"The bees do not harm us. We work among them all the time"." Saecar spat at the ground. "We," he jerked his head at his dead friend on the ground, "have encountered the bees at the edge of our territory while hunting. They have a large hive located on the western branch of the Snake River, built into the bank of the dried riverbed. We are blessed by our ancestors and protected from them."

"If that is the case, why are you trying to kill us?" asked Mitch.

"And why do you care what we do with the bees in the facility?" asked Pam.

"The bees are sacred," said Lippac. "The bees *are* our ancestors."

Pam and Mitch exchanged glances. "And this is confirmed, how? Does the chief believe this also?"

Lippac and Saecar nodded in affirmation.

"Geez, Saecar, why didn't you just tell us this?" said Pam, lowering her gun. "We are on the same side, you know. We have no wish to harm the bees or the ancestors. But we do need to understand what has happened. There is room for all of us to work together here." She walked over to Saecar. "I apologize for any offense I have caused. It was not intentional." She knelt in front of him, gazing into his eyes. "Can you believe me? I have no wish to harm any of you." Pam's eyes hardened as she stared at the young warrior. "But I cannot allow you free if you are only going to attack us once again. There is no time for this foolishness, and innocent people may get hurt."

Saecar's eyes shifted to his dead friend for a moment. "Dromid died a warrior's death. Do not dishonour him by attributing innocence to his passing. He knew what he was about." Saecar's eyes met Pam's once again, and he gave a terse nod.

"I will hear it from your lips," she said. "Swear on your warrior's heart that you will cause us no further harm."

"I swear that we will not stand in your way in this matter unless you bring harm to the tribe. Then our first duty is to the Seiko, not to you."

"Agreed." Pam glanced over her shoulder at Lippac. "Do you also swear?"

"I swear."

Pam stood. "Untie them, Mitch."

Mitch stood, his eyes passing between the three. "Are you sure?"

"Yes, I am sure. A warrior's oath is sacred. They will not go back on their word."

Mitch shrugged, not sharing Pam's confidence, then bent to untie the warriors.

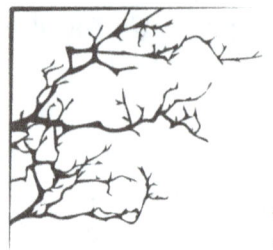

Chapter 11
Runaway Alexa

ALEXA SLIPPED IN TO the mechanic's garage, leaving the roll-up door wide open, about four feet off the ground. She had spied her ride in the dim interior when she had driven past the closed shop with an injured Peet in the back seat. Now, she returned to the building. It had taken some prying with her swiped hammer, but the door had finally given way, and she stood in the dusty interior, letting her eyes adjust to the shade. The garage had the feel of a museum or maybe the Rapture. Tools and tool chests lay open and scattered about on work benches, as though the men and women who had been working there had left for lunch and were about to return. The inch-thick coat of dust gave away the truth, however. Everyone quit on the same day, and the owner had locked the doors and walked away.

In the corner sat a lawn mower. It was an old riding lawn mower, but still...if it worked it would mean transportation. The mower was a dull red colour and coated in grey dust. Dried grass clippings clung to the mower deck, the consistency of straw. As Alexa moved, dust motes swirled into the air, shimmering in the weak light shining down from the fixed window panes. Alexa ran over to the machine and wiped the dust off the seat with her hand, then climbed on board. The keys were in the ignition. Smiling with glee, she turned the key. Nothing happened. She tried again, holding it in the start position, but all was silent. The gauges shifted though, so she knew the battery had power.

Puzzled, she hopped off the tractor and pulled on the seat. It swung up on hinges to reveal the battery. On the underside of the seat was a diagram showing how to start the tractor. The image showed a seated person pushing on a floor clutch. Avalon put the seat back down and then climbed back onto the split vinyl covering then pressed down on the silver button on the floor and turned the key. The tractor whined but did not catch. Avalon got off once again and twisted off the knob for the gas tank. She could not see any gas and the float was way down the tube.

Alexa wandered around the garage, looking for a jerry can of gasoline. Her eyes locked on a high shelf where she saw a red plastic container tucked back into a corner behind some machine parts. She climbed up the outside of the shelving and reached for the can. It was heavy. She placed it on a lower shelf and then climbed down one level at a time, shifting the can at each level until she was back to the cement. Grabbing the container, she hurried back to the lawn tractor. She pulled out the plastic fill nozzle and took a sniff. It was gasoline. She filled the tank to the brim then closed the jerry can, tying it on the back of the tractor. The extra fuel would be needed.

Jumping back in the seat, she depressed the clutch then turned the key. Nothing happened. She tried again, and then again, and on the fourth turn of the key, the engine caught and the lawn tractor roared to life. Black smoke billowed out the exhaust, and the tractor rattled as she shoved it into low gear. She drove forward slowly as she weaved in and out of the detritus stacked through the garage. She cut her turn short, and the mower deck plowed into a stand with tools on it, sending them crashing to the floor. She swiped a bag of wrenches as she drove past the mechanic's chest and placed it on her lap before she roared out of the opening. Once free of the garage, she put the lawn mower in to high gear and drove down the laneway past the house and into the field at the back. Cross-country would be much faster than sticking to the roads, and she could see the church at the edge of town, the cross on the spire clearly visible over the low brush marking the divide between abandoned fields.

She was out in the open, anyone could see her, but she could also see anyone approaching, so safety was guaranteed at least until she got closer to her objective. She knew the way to the cache of medical supplies, once she reached the church. The route was a familiar one and she planned to stash the riding lawn mower in a place only she would find it. The machine bucked under her on the uneven ground, and she rocked as she steered, thinking through her plan.

Alexa was excited at the thought of finally seeing Gabriel again. He really did look like Nivens, so the name fit. He had the same distracted air and his eyes would grow so large when worried. He was super funny, too. She laughed so much when she was around him. She didn't care so much for his older brother, but she would put up with him to be able to spend time with Gabriel.

The stash was located in the base of the church, of all things. The church was not abandoned; in fact, it was still very much operational. They ran a spartan soup kitchen in the church, but with food in such short supply, the hours were sporadic. A sign would go out on the street and the line ups would start almost immediately. The food would be gone within two hours. But the sign really wasn't needed. The smell of the food cooking would be enough to gather a crowd.

Alexa hoped that tomorrow would not be a soup kitchen day, although the crowd might hide her. She nervously nibbled on her lower lip as she thought about her plan. She would sleep tonight by the dry well and hide the tractor under the rotting bale of hay. She could climb under the hay as well. It would keep the nighttime chill off, too. Her backpack bounced on her back as she went over a big bump. It was mostly empty so that she could carry the medical supplies back to Peet.

Alexa traveled for two hours without incident. The sun stroked its way to the horizon, swimming through the shimmering late-day haze, which darkened to purple as she arrived at her chosen campsite. The abandoned farmhouse was a pile of burnt rubble, the victim of a vandal's fire several years ago. The barn had collapsed with age and grass grew through the twisted wood beams. The metal roofing had been scavenged long ago. The barn looked like the bones of a dragon, bleaching under an unforgiving sun. She bypassed the buildings and pulled around the back side of the barn, where several round bales were stacked, and pulled up beside the hay. She turned off the lawn mower and the roar died. She would need to let it cool down as the exhaust was too hot to go under the bales.

She got off the mower and wandered over to the well. A metal pipe with a long handle stood over the well cap. Alexa slid the pack from her back and then unzipped it, sliding her hand inside to search for her water bottle. She flipped the lid then took a swig. She was very thirsty. She gulped two swallows of the liquid and then placed the bottle under the spout and began pumping the handle. It creaked and screeched, stiff with disuse. Every time she stopped at the old farm, she tried the well, and every time it came up dry. The pump stuck, and she put the bottle down on the cement lid then took the handle in both hands and shoved with all her weight. The lever resisted her efforts. She pushed it up to eye level then pulled down, and with a twang it shifted. The whole pump shifted and the handle dropped. Surprised, she stumbled and nearly fell. Alexa straightened and moved the handle. Now it moved with ease, up and down, with hardly any resistance at all. Grinning, she pumped up and down, and slowly resistance built. She reached down and grabbed her water bottle as a gush of water exploded from the end of the pipe. It was short lived. A half-dozen strokes later, the water trickled away, but it was enough to fill her bottle and dunk her dusty face underneath, before the water stopped flowing.

She carried the precious liquid back to the haystack. She screwed the lid on tight then grabbed her pack and burrowed into the hay bale to create a nest for herself. She crawled back out and pushed the tractor up against it then pulled down a bunch of the loose cuttings to hide the tractor. She crawled back inside the spoiled hay and settled down to rest. She drew the top of her shirt over her nose to filter the dust while she slept.

In the morning, she would get the supplies Peet needed. Alexa mulled over her plans as she settled down to sleep, watching the day fade to night. She did not want anyone to know she had been near the church. A young girl alone on the streets of Solace was begging for more trouble than she could handle. The times she had left the barn on the Gainsborough Manor, she had made sure she was never seen, not by Avalon, not by anyone. Except for Gabe. Thoughts of Gabe made her smile, and she drifted off to sleep with his face in her mind.

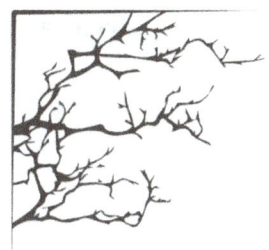

Chapter 12
Contagion

AVALON SHIFTED ON HER sweat-soaked bed, thrashing. Cramps ran up and down her legs, locking her legs in a rigor-mortis-like slab of agony. She opened her mouth to cry out, but no sound escaped the open cavity. She pried her eyelids open. A sticky film coated her lashes, gluing the lids closed. She tried to scrub her fist across her eyes, but her hands and arms were tied down, restricting motion. From the dim recess of her feverish mind, she acknowledged that she had been stung and that she was likely dying in the same fashion as the bodies they had seen in the warehouse. Unable to relieve her pain, she fled back into the dark recesses of her mind and hid from the torture.

A hum, like the fluttering of tiny wings, filled her ears. Thousands of them filled her mind until the sound became a thrumming purr, the pulse point of a thousand sensations. Avalon focused on the hum, sinking into the white noise and submerging her pain, sacrificing her will to the fire coursing through her veins. There, she floated in a haze, time having no meaning. She must have dozed off, but she really wasn't sure. Avalon thought she felt a hand on her brow, and then her jaw opened and water flowed past her cracked lips. She sucked in the liquid, grateful for the flow of cooling water down her throat. A voice murmured, but it made no sense. All she could hear was the thrum of the wings. It drowned out all other sound. A prick on her arm barely registered, and she drifted off to sleep.

TRENCH WATCHED AS THE cramps eased and Avalon relaxed into unconsciousness. He let out the breath he hadn't realized he was holding. Avalon had been gagging on her own tongue when he came into the room, what he thought was an impossible feat with a ventilator in place. Cris was nowhere to be seen.

Cursing, he had flung himself down on the thrashing girl and forced his fingers between her clenched teeth, forcing her jaw apart. He pulled her tongue out of the way and then poured a dribble of water down her throat to ease her swallowing reflex. Plunging the needle of oxycodone into her arm, he counted while he waited for the drug to take effect. She relaxed under his hands, and he finally felt he could take his hands away.

Avalon was a mess. The boils on her skin had burst, soaking the sheets. She seemed unaware of them, but her palms were dry and the skin white. She was dehydrating, and he needed to keep fluids in her. That was what Cris was supposed to be doing while he was gone. Fuming, he craned his neck to see out the door. There was no motion.

His gaze returned to Avalon. His eyes wandered over her still form. Below her left ear, where the bee had stung her, was a blotch of skin. He squinted at the spot. *Is that a bee? I must be tired.* He rubbed his tired eyes and then peered closer at the mark. *It is a bee.* Not taking his eyes off Avalon, Trench reached inside his pocket and pulled out the vial of oxycodone that he'd intended to use to top up Avalon's dose. He plunged the needle into the rubbing alcohol jar by her bedside then shook it dry before pushing the needle through the rubber seal. He drew up a shot of the painkiller then rolled up his sleeve and plunged it into his arm. He winced at the sting. Once it was empty, he put the bottle on table and the needle back in the rubbing alcohol jar. Then, he stretched out beside Avalon on the bed with his back to her.

As he relaxed, he realized that he might be exposing himself to whatever was making her ill, but he didn't care. When he woke, he would search for more answers, but the best source of answers was lying beside him. He wanted to be with her when she woke, and he couldn't rely on the other gang members to care or watch over her. They were too concerned about catching whatever she had. It was a miracle they brought her back at all. He didn't think she was contagious. There was no evidence to support that. But something was happening with Avalon, and he intended to find out what it was. His eyes drooped as the oxycodone took effect despite his attempts to fight off the encroaching oblivion. He blinked several times, and then he slid into a dreamless sleep.

AVALON WOKE WITH A start. Someone was in the room with her. She could smell them. She wiggled on the bed, testing her limbs, and the minute she started to move, images flashed into her head, faster than she could process them in her weakened state. She tried to push them away, but she couldn't. The visions came faster and faster, and panic flooded her body. She opened her mouth to scream, but something was lodged in her throat. She flexed her arms but could not move them, either. A keening, high-pitched whine escaped her throat as terror took over her panic. Her eyes opened to a blurry grey. She wailed again and then felt the bed shift beside her. A face entered her vision. She thought she knew him, but he was weirdly distorted, as though being viewed from the wrong end of a telescope. His face was concave and rounded. Avalon's eyes widened, and she turned her head away. A voice reached out to her, familiar and reassuring. She turned her head slowly toward the sound.

"Avalon. It's me, Trench. Understand? It's Trench."

Avalon stared at the distortion and nodded.

"You have been very sick. I had to put a tube in your throat to keep you from dying. That is why you can't swallow." Avalon nodded again. "You were trying to pull it out, so we tied you down. I need to take the tube out. I am going to leave you tied until I have it out, OK? Are you ready to do this?" Avalon's eyes widened with fear, but then she nodded.

Trench got up and left the room then returned with a basin and a pitcher of warm salt water rinse. He sat down beside Avalon then placed a gentle hand on hers. "I will try to be gentle, but this is going to hurt. You will feel better when it is out. Ready?" A terse nod accompanied his words. "OK, here goes."

Trench took hold of the end of the tube and gently began to extract it from her throat. Avalon's eyes bulged at the sensation. She stared blindly at where she thought Trench's face to be located. Tensed against the sensation, she strained at her bonds. The cords bit into her wrists and ankles. A strangled whimper escaped her lips, but Trench focused on removing the tube. It slipped free of her throat, and he dumped it into the basin, and then poured salt water into a glass.

"I am going to untie you, then I need you to gargle with the salt water. Do not swallow it, just gargle and spit, OK?"

She nodded, gingerly testing her swallow reflex. Trench untied her hands and feet and helped her to a sitting position. She opened her mouth to speak, but he put a finger to his lips to stop her.

"Don't speak yet. Let's get the rinse going.

Avalon took the glass in shaky hands and lifted it to her mouth. The salt stung and tears formed in her eyes. She swished it around her mouth then spat it out into the basin. She took another sip, then gagged on the water and spat it out with such force that it splashed on-to Trench's arms and face.

"Hey, easy there!" he said, wiping off the fluids with the corner of the sheet.

"Trench?" Avalon croaked. "I can't see you. Why can't I see?"

Trench paused, a worried frown creasing his brow. He leaned in closer to Avalon. "I am right here." He picked up her hands and placed them on his face. "See? It's me."

He placed his hands on her face, peeling back an eyelid to examine her pupils. Her eyes appeared normal, except for an opaque film that almost seemed like an extra eyelid. Puzzled, he released her face.

"I don't know what is going on here, Avalon, but you have had a very severe reaction to the bee sting. The only thing I can think of is that the oxycodone has somehow protected you from the deadly effects. But there are side effects occurring that we will have to figure out as we go along. I thought you were going to die at one point." His voice caught for a moment, and he cleared his throat. "I won't let that happen. That was a very brave thing you did. You saved Magnum and Cris. They owe you their lives."

Avalon swayed as a wave of dizziness washed over her.

"You need to rest. Perhaps you can sleep better now that the tube is out."

Avalon nodded and lay back down on the cot.

"I will check back on you in a few hours and bring some food."

Avalon nodded again in affirmation, her throat too sore for words.

Trench walked out of the room, closing the door behind him. Once he was out of sight, he looked down at his hands. His skin was burning where it had come in contact with Avalon's saliva. Blisters were forming. He hurried over to the kitchen sink and washed his skin under the cold water, but the blisters continued to grow.

Avalon is contagious. I hope I am right about the oxycodone. On that grim thought, he set about preparing some food. If he was also infected, then he needed to quarantine himself along with Avalon and they would need supplies. He had a feeling he was about to get to know Avalon very well.

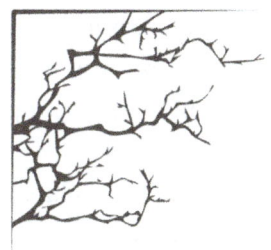

Chapter 13
Blessings

ALEXA CREPT UP ALONG the low stone wall that framed the gardens at the rear of the church. Dried grasses crunched underfoot as she ran in a half crouch along the structure, staying hidden from the throng of people that waited out front of the church for the doors to open. It was as large of a crowd as she had ever seen lined up for food. Knowing that the fights usually broke out around the time the doors opened, Alexa hurried to the exterior cellar doors. As she crept closer, she spied a familiar face. Smiling, she raised her hand in greeting. Alexa closed the distance between them and popped down beside his kneeling form.

"Heya, Gabe."

"Heya, Alexa." Gabe ran his fingers through his mop of dark hair, pushing the curls out of his eyes. Slender and tall for fourteen years of age, he exuded an aura of confidence. "The priest knows we are here. I heard the bolt click back on the doors a few minutes ago. Come on."

He grabbed her hand and pulled her along behind him, crossing the few feet separating them. Reaching the slanted doors, he grabbed the right handle and pulled. The door opened to reveal a staircase descending into the ground. They scurried down the steps, pulling the door closed behind them and bolting it from the inside. At the base of the stairs, they flipped the wall switch, illuminating the windowless room. Metal shelving lined the walls, filled with boxes of supplies for

Sunday services. They hurried past the boxes to a smaller room with a glass door. They pushed open this door and entered a room outfitted with a small kitchen. Shabby folding chairs sat around a matching metal table. A fridge and stove sat side by side on the end wall with a small counter wedged between the two appliances. Cupboards lined the right wall.

Gabe began opening cupboards to see what was inside. Alexa knew what she was looking for and went straight for the last upper cupboard where she found the medications and supplies that Dr. Song needed so badly to treat Peet.

"Oxycodone, bandages, alcohol wipes, needles...." She listed off the supplies as she put them into a bag, taking more than was strictly needed but hedging her bets that they wouldn't go to waste.

"Alexa, Avalon is sick." Gabe's voice filled the room, a deep baritone that broke midway through. The child's voice came and went within the same sentence. "We believe she has been stung by the bees that the government is experimenting with."

Alexa's back stiffened, and she whirled around to face him with alarm on her face.

"No!" Terror flashed over her face. "The bees kill. Why didn't you tell me this sooner? Where is she? Is she with you?"

"No, she is with the Firebrand gang. They snuck into a warehouse that we used to house supplies in. A couple months ago, the feds arrived and took it over. They began pulling people off the street. We got wind of it. Rather than start a full-scale war with the government, we sold our 'protection services' to them to act as lookouts and keep the warehouse secure. It was ours anyways, but," he shrugged, "it seemed better this way. Avalon and a couple of other Firebrands arrived a couple days ago and snuck into the warehouse but were cornered by the feds. They got away, but we saw her collapse in an alley. The bees are loose in the warehouse. We don't dare open a door. We can see them swarming the windows, trying to get out. We are planning to burn the building to the ground."

"When?" Alexa grabbed her bag of supplies and pushed it into her backpack.

"Tonight," said Gabriel.

"I need to get these supplies back to Peet, but they will want to know where the Firebrand gang is so they can go to Avalon. Do you know where their headquarters are?"

"Yeah, I could lead you there easy enough."

"Will you help me find it?"

"Sure." His lips twisted into a tense smile.

A large crash sounded from upstairs and then the sound of hundreds of feet pounded over their heads. A muffled voice shouted instructions, then other voices rose in anger. Alexa and Gabe exchanged looks.

"We need to get out of here," said Gabe. "Come on."

He grabbed her hand and dragged her back toward the cellar doors just as a door opened at the far end of the basement.

"Who left this light on?" grumbled a voice as Alexa and Gabe ran to the doors and slid the bolt, unlocking the cellar door to the outside.

They slipped past and quietly lowered it then ran off to hide behind the wall. They heard the bolt slip back into place. It was an old game, one they had played many times with the old friar. He made sure that the street gangs had the medical supplies they needed in exchange for some extra muscle on soup kitchen day when the hungry throngs teetered on the edge of violence. The Imbroglio gang's protection of the church was recognized by the throng, and no one wanted to cross the gang members.

Gabe whistled softly as they ran out through the back gate and answering whistles followed their flight. Once clear of the crowds, they ran through the overgrown park and out the back end of town, toward the abandoned farm and the lawn tractor that would take them back to

Peet much faster than walking. They reached the tractor about thirty minutes later. Gabe sat in the seat and set Alexa on his knee, and they were quickly on their way.

Alexa couldn't wipe the grin off her face. She had acquired the needed supplies, and she had the best seat in the house, as far as she was concerned, on Gabe's knee. It was a good day, for sure. She giggled, and Gabe gave her a shy smile. Ripped jeans or no, he was the most handsome man she had ever seen.

Three hours later, they roared into the lane at the back of Dr. Song's house, bouncing through the ruts to the house. Dr. Song stepped out onto his back porch, a shotgun in hand. Gabe cut the engine, and they allowed the sound to die before Alexa called out.

"It's me, Dr. Song! I went to get medical supplies."

Hearing her voice, the gun lowered. A voice roared through the open door.

"Alexa, I am going to tan your hide for scaring me like that. Get in here, right now!"

Alexa grinned and took Gabe's hand. "Come on, his bark is worse than his bite."

Together, they entered the house, a frowning Dr. Song following them inside. Alexa gave Dr. Song a hug as she passed him and he grunted, his eyes never leaving Gabe. Gabe walked cautiously behind Alexa, giving Dr. Song no reason to level his gun.

"Alexa! Get in here!" Peet bellowed from the couch.

Alexa skipped into the room and ran over to Peet to give him a hug. "I'm here, see?"

"I wish I had my pa's belt. I would soon teach you to sneak away like that. Time you had some proper supervision. Sneaking off like that, you gave us heart attacks!"

Alexa directed her best 'tween' pout at him, which was halfway between a lip tremble and a smirk.

"You let Avalon go do what she wants. And I am the age she was, when we were first left alone. Besides, I have been going out on my own for a couple years now. Do you really think I just sat in that old barn by myself all this time? This is Gabe," she said, pulling Gabe forward by the hand. "He is part of the Imbroglio gang, and a good friend. He can help us. He wants to help us. We have supplies, see?"

She upended her pack on the floor as Dr. Song sank into his chair. Medical supplies tumbled onto the floor. Dr. Song's eyes inventoried the loot.

"That is quite the haul, Alexa, and appreciated. But you see, I have more supplies here. I only keep what I need in my bag. You didn't need to risk yourself to get them. Next time, let us know of your plans. We need to work together. If you know of a source of medical supplies, then we can be more specific on what you collect."

Alexa blushed, her ears turning red. Chastised, she mumbled "OK. Maybe you are right."

Gabe spoke into the embarrassed silence. "Alexa did well. She is resourceful and smart. She also knows her medications. We'd recruit her to the Imbroglio, but she is too loyal to her sister. Speaking of which, Avalon has been stung."

"Oh shit," said Peet, grimacing. "That girl! Where is she? We must go help her."

Dr. Song nodded. "If she has been stung, she has but days. No one survives longer than a week. Where is she?"

"She is being cared for at the Firebrand's headquarters, an underground restaurant called Frankie's Finger Foods," said Gabe. "I can show you where it is. I know the safest routes in and out of the city center. Better yet, I can make sure your car is still there when you want to leave."

Gabe slouched, pushing the flop of curls back off his forehead. His ripped jeans were soiled and his T-shirt plastered to his back with sweat, but despite his grubby appearance, Dr. Song liked him.

"Son, if you would like to take a shower before we go, please help yourself. Bathroom is on the right. Water is set to a five-minute timer and shuts off automatically, so be quick about it. There are towels in the cupboard behind the door."

Gabe nodded, grateful, and headed down the hall to the indicated door.

Peet watched the skinny lad disappear behind the bathroom door. "Nice kid. I like him." He shifted on the couch, grimacing. "Now hand me my pants so I can get dressed." Dr. Song tossed his clothes to him. "Alexa, go pack some drinks and food. You don't want to see this."

Giggling, Alexa ran out of the living room as instructed.

Ten minutes later, they were all assembled in the living room, and they trooped out the door to Peet's waiting sedan. Dr. Song had washed the interior upholstery, cleaning away the bloodstains, but a tinny smell lingered in the air when they opened the doors. Alexa wrinkled her nose as she climbed into the back seat with Gabe.

"Hey, I took a shower!" said Gabe, grinning at Alexa.

Dr. Song helped Peet into the passenger seat and took the wheel, starting the engine with a flip of the wrist. He steered the car down the lane and out onto the main road. Alexa felt a thump of anxiety at the familiar scenery passing by her window, remembering her last panicked trip down the same road. Gabe bumped her shoulder, and she leaned over to whisper in his hear.

"Can you really get us into the Firebrand gang without us all dying? They don't allow people on their turf, especially Imbroglio gang members."

"Yeah," he whispered back. "I am one of the few who can talk to them. My brother sends me when the two factions need to talk. They will not harm anyone under sixteen."

He smiled, and Alexa thought the dimple on his cheek was adorable.

"Which way, Gabe?" Peet's gruff voice broke into their musings.

"Take the exit for the city center. After crossing the Burgoyne Bridge, turn right and left at the brickworks. Once you reach the projects, pull over by Garden Alley Five. Dumb name. Never were any gardens planted in the alleys."

They travelled in silence for about thirty minutes. They passed only one car on the highway and only lightweight, fuel efficient motorcycles, once they got off at the exit. Most people did not use their cars unless absolutely necessary, as gasoline supplies came into the city once a week, and then the trucks were accompanied by an armed escort. Most gas stations had electrified perimeter fencing in place and the driver had to prepay outside the gate before they were allowed inside to pump gas. Armed security was present day and night. They drove past one of the stations, and the guards watched them drive by with their hands on their guns, suspicious of their intentions. Their narrowed eyes did not leave the car until they turned the corner at the old brickworks.

"This is it. Pull over here." Gabe pointed to a fire hydrant. The caps were missing, having been removed a long time ago to search for water. Someone had spray-painted it to look like a city worker pissing on the sidewalk. A puddle of paint was sprayed on the sidewalk in bright yellow. As soon as they pulled up to the curb, twenty teens melted out of the shadows and surrounded the car.

"Stay here for a minute. I will talk to them." Gabe opened his door and got out, walking over to a solid girl of about eighteen, who looked ready to hit him.

Alexa reached for the door handle to get out, but Peet's voice halted her.

"Stay put. Let him do his thing. Wait."

Alexa hesitated and then sank back on the cushion, watching Gabe with anxious eyes. The girl laughed and the gang members followed suit, but Gabe waved his hands and gestured toward where the Imbroglio's territorial lines intersected those of the Firebrand. His lips moved, and then he pointed at the alley. The girl frowned then spoke to a blond-haired girl. She nodded, and the gang parted, allowing the two girls to approach the car. Peet's door was pulled opened.

"Follow us," said Magnum.

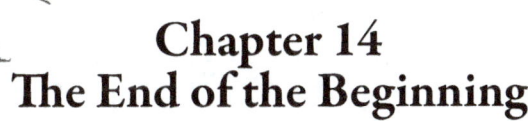

Chapter 14
The End of the Beginning

MAGNUM LED THEM DOWN the staircase into Frankie's Finger Foods and back through the restaurant to the kitchens. Peet's limp was more pronounced by the time they reached the swinging door, and he paused for a moment to lean on the door frame. Alexa, noticing that he had stopped walking, hurried back to him.

"Peet, you need to sit down. You are still weak. You lost too much blood." She took his arm and tugged him toward a chair back in the restaurant, but he brushed her hand off of his arm, swaying slightly.

"Not until I see Avalon," he growled then straightened and followed Dr. Song's retreating back.

They snaked around the grimy countertops and past peeling painted walls to the back of the kitchen. The second half of the kitchen was dark, as was the room where Avalon was being treated. Magnum stopped then spun on Cris, who nearly bumped into her.

"Weren't you supposed to be watching Avalon? Making sure she was cared for? Why were you out on the street today?"

Cris gave Magnum a disgusted look. "Would you want to be around someone stung by those bees? Who knows what the side effects are? I told Trench I would only stay as long as I felt it was safe. When her skin erupted in blisters, I left. I have no desire to be near someone like that. You all should have done what I said. She should have died on the street and the disease along with her."

Alexa pushed her way up to the two girls, Gabe at her shoulder. "You would have let my sister die?"

Cris spared a fraction of a glance at the younger Gainsborough then said, "In a heartbeat. She will be the death of us all now." She grabbed Magnum by the sleeve. "It's not too late, you know," she whispered.

The sound of a gun's safety being removed filled the room like a glass shattering on cement. The sound was echoed by six other guns, and a tense silence shivered through the room.

"There will be no shooting." Peet's hand was steady as he leaned back against the door frame, his gun pointed at the pair of girls. All five guns pointed back at him, but he paid them no mind.

Magnum glared at Peet. "You dare bear your firearm inside the headquarters of the Firebrand? Are you insane?"

"Perhaps. Or maybe I am just too old to care about your little turf wars. I am here to get Avalon, and I will bring her out of here alive. The question is, how many of you are willing to die to prevent that? Is it really worth your life when your leader has seen fit to save her?" He waved his gun in the direction of the dark. "Now, go turn on the lights so we can see what the hell we are dealing with here."

"Put those away!" snapped Magnum, glaring at the others. "And keep your mouth shut, Cris. No one is going to save your backside again."

When the guns disappeared into pockets once again, she turned her back on everyone and walked to the back wall to flip the switches. The back half of the restaurant lit up.

Dr. Song, who had stepped out of the line of fire, hurried over to the back office, which was still in the dark. The blinds were pulled. On the door, a sign had been taped, written in a rough male handwriting, the strokes bold and sharp. "*Warning! Do not enter. Occupants are con-*

tagious. Trench." Dr. Song turned on the light from the switch located by the door. The room was bathed in a weak light from the single overhead bulb. Trench and Avalon lay sleeping on the bed, covered in blisters. Their chests rose and fell, the breathing laboured. Dr. Song sighed, the sound a low groan as it passed his lips.

"No one will be moving these two."

He took his hand away from the doorknob. Before he could react, Alexa and Gabe had gripped the handle and opened the door, stepping inside the room. Dr. Song gasped then pulled the door shut.

"Alexa, what have you done?" he shouted, furious.

Alexa looked back at him, not understanding his concern. Then her eyes fell on the back side of the taped message. She could read the message in reverse as the marker shone through the glass. Peet was just behind them but Dr. Song grabbed him by the shoulders and pushed him back.

"No one is to enter this room!" he shouted. "It is quarantine. Magnum, you need to place a twenty-four-hour guard at all times on this door. *Do as I say*!" he yelled at the startled girls. "Peet. You can't help them. Now back away."

For an elderly man, he had surprising strength, and Peet staggered as he was shoved hard.

"I can't just leave them there! We have to help them. That is why we came, dammit!"

"You can't help them if you are dead. Now, sit."

Peet sank into a chair by the door, his mouth sagging with misery.

Alexa and Gabe turned their backs on the watchers and moved over to the side of the bed. Alexa reached over and gave Avalon's shoulder a quick shake. "Avalon, wake up. It's me, Alexa. Avalon, wake up!"

Avalon groaned, and slowly her eyes opened. She blinked several times then said in a husky voice that sounded like crumpled paper, "Alexa? Is that you?"

"Yeah, it's me. Can't you see me? I am standing right here."

Avalon squinted at her then put a hand over her eyes. "The light hurts. Can you turn the light out?"

"OK." Alexa went over to the door. "Turn off the light. 'It's hurting their eyes."

Dr. Song nodded, and the light went out. He crowded in close to the glass to peer inside the room.

"Is that better?"

"Yeah. You shouldn't be in here."

"I had to see you. They said you were dying."

"I might still be dying. And now you will, too." She swallowed heavily, throat dry. "Water."

Alexa handed her the glass of water sitting on the stand, and Avalon took a small drink. "Under the bed, med kit. You must take a shot right now, both of you. Oxycodone. Hurry. Only thing that might save you," she rasped past a throat that was like sandpaper.

Alexa reached under the bed and pulled out a tool box filled with medication and bandages. She drew a shot of oxycodone for both her and Gabe then walked over to the door to show Dr. Song the amount. When he nodded that it was the proper dose, she administered the shot to both herself and Gabe. Avalon sat still on the bed, swaying.

"Tell them to bring you two sleeping bags for the floor. You are not leaving until you are better. Your fate will be the same as mine. You should have stayed away."

"Our fates were always tied together, Avalon. I love you. We will get through this, together, as we always have."

Avalon smiled at her words.

"Who is your friend?" said Avalon.

Gabe introduced himself. Trench stirred. He opened his eyes, blinking steadily, raising his hands to rub them with his blistered fists.

"I can't see. Avalon, are you there?" Trench swayed, and then he vomited, spewing sick over the side of the bed. Most of it hit the bowl he had placed there but some did not. With a groan he laid back down, his head hanging over the side. Alexa got the bucket of salted water and began mopping up the sick. She emptied the basin in the toilet of the spartan, ensuite bathroom and returned with the clean vessel, placing it back on the floor.

"You are both about to get very, very sick. None of us can leave this room, not while we are ill.

"I brought a doctor with me. Dr. Song knows all about the bee illness. He can help." Alexa pointed to the anxious looking Dr. Song who hovered by the door.

Avalon got to her feet and staggered to the door. "Hello, Dr. Song. Hopefully you can help us. No one must come in this room. We have supplies and food. There is one thing that we need, though. Raw honeycomb. Can you find some?"

"Raw honeycomb? That is a very rare thing indeed. But I think I know where some might be located." He stared at Avalon, fascinated. "How is it that you have so far survived your encounter with the bees?"

Avalon gave him a tired smile. "I am not sure, but I feel an urge to find honeycomb. The whole comb, wax and all. There is something in it that will help us, I am sure of it. Oh, and get us something to sleep on, for the floor."

Dr. Song nodded. "It will be as you ask, Avalon. We will scour the county until we find some. In the meantime, keep those three alive." He turned away and called to the room. Two boys ran off in search of bedding.

Avalon nodded her thanks and pushed away from the door, staggering back to the bed. One way or another, she would see that they all lived through this. She felt different, changed. She had been changed by the illness. It was only now that she had the strength to begin sorting through her trial to see what the effects had been. She had lots of time to sort it out. She was going nowhere soon.

Before she could settle onto the bed, Gabe moaned then crashed to the floor, thrashing. Alexa quivered and sat down on the floor beside him, shaking. A trace of fear crossed her face before she made it vanish.

There was a knock on the door and then everyone backed away to the other side of the kitchen. Avalon opened the door, picked up the blankets and pillows and then closed it again. She made up a bed on the floor at the foot of the cot and rolled Gabe onto the sheets. Alexa mopped his fevered brow with a damp cloth. With a groan, she lay down beside him and began to shake with tremors as the infection spread in her system.

Avalon climbed back onto her bed and collapsed. It was going to be a long few days or weeks. She didn't know for sure. Her last thought before sinking back into unconciousness was that she was going to make the government pay.

One way or another, they would pay for their crimes. She would make sure of it.

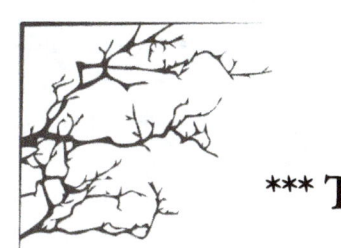

*** THE END ***

If you have loved reading these first four books of The Silent Lands Chronicles, please consider leaving a review on Amazon! Your reviews are precious to us and help us continue to find a cure for this dying land ☺. Join our mailing list[1] and never miss a new release!

---

1. http://susanfaw.com/sendy/edit-list?i=1&l=9

This series is ongoing. Check back soon for further installments in this epic eco-dystopian adventure series!

***

THE SILENT LANDS CHRONICLES
By E.A. Darl
STEALING SILENCE
SEEKING SILENCE
STINGING SILENCE
SHADOWED SILENCE

By Judith Docken
GHOSTED

By Sylva Fae
RAINBOW MONSTERS

MINDFUL MONSTERS
CHILDREN'S CHRISTMAS COLLECTION

THE SPIRIT SHIELD SAGA
Susan Faw
SOUL SURVIVOR
SEER OF SOULS
SOUL SANCTUARY
SOUL SACRIFICE

THE HEART OF THE CITADEL
HEART OF DESTINY
HEART OF TYR
HEART OF SHADRA

Don't miss out!

Visit the website below and you can sign up to receive emails whenever Susan Faw publishes a new book. There's no charge and no obligation.

https://books2read.com/r/B-A-UXAD-FXDR

BOOKS 2 READ

Connecting independent readers to independent writers.

www.ingramcontent.com/pod-product-compliance
Lightning Source LLC
Chambersburg PA
CBHW070803120626
46557CB00002B/700